BLOOD
FOR
FREEDOM

On a Mission among the Mayas

J. P. Piché

Order this book online on Amazon

For information, contact the author's publisher: The Moving Words LLC, 855 McCloud St., Santa Maria, CA, 93455, info@themovingwords.com.

Because of the dynamic nature of the Internet, any web addresses or links contained in this book may have changed since publication and may no longer be valid. The views expressed in this work are solely those of the author and do not necessarily reflect the views of the publisher, and the publisher hereby disclaims any responsibility for them.

Any resemblance to existing persons is coincidental. The actions of the historical figures are partly of public knowledge, partly of imagination.

Front and back cover illustration/Getty Images.

www.themovingwords.com
www.bloodforfreedom.com
J. P. Piché: satjeev@videotron.ca

This is for Céline and Yvette

The Theology of Liberation

"Sin may also be of institutional nature. When social, economic, and political structures are violating human rights, reducing each other's humanity, or forcing people to live in inhumane conditions, the Church has an obligation to denounce and condemn those structures and it is the right of the people to alter or abolish them."

Gustavo Guttiérrez

Table of Contents

Prologue

Having moved dangerously far from the coast, the Quetzal bird now let himself be carried by the air currents blowing over the ocean towards the temple of Tulum, a Mayan fortress perched on a rocky cliff overlooking the Caribbean Sea. Seeing the temple silhouette in the distance, the prospect of returning to his natural habitat in the Petén jungle gave him new strength, and he quickly passed over the ancient building.

Now flying above the forest canopy, he could soon make out the roof crest of the highest pyramid at the Mayan site of Tikal rising above the treetops, the last landmark before his destination. The whistling of the wind in his ears was gradually drowned out by a haunting drumbeat and the roar of a large crowd.

On top of the giant structure, just below the crest, he saw two Mayan priests in ceremonial costumes grab a woman dressed in a white tunic by her arms and force her to lie down on her back on a sacrificial altar. A third priest wearing a jaguar headed mask and a feather bonnet emerged from an opening under the crest and stepped to the edge of the terrace before the hysterical crowd. The crowd became silent and fell to their knees when they saw the latter brandishing a long flint knife.

For a moment, only a drumbeat sounding like the heartbeat of Mother Earth could be heard.

When the priest turned to face the woman on the altar, the Quetzal understood that he was about to cut out her heart before the two other priests throw her body down the high steps. At that precise moment, the shadow of the bird loomed over them, and the woman looked up, showing her blue painted face. The tears running down her cheeks had drawn stripes that revealed the original whiteness of her skin. As soon as he recognized her, the Quetzal lost his ability to fly and fell.

Paul Desilets woke up with a start, in a state of shock in his plane seat, all his senses on alert, feeling his heart beating in his throat. It took him a few seconds to realize he had been dreaming, that in his dream he had turned into a Quetzal bird. He could still hear a hissing sound in his ears, even after swallowing his saliva to relieve the pressure in his ears. He had fallen asleep reading a traveling book with the Quetzal bird (the national emblem of Guatemala) on the cover. The book was still resting on his lap.

The woman he had dreamed of was Louise, the fiancée he had said farewell to before leaving his hometown for working as an aid worker with the Mayas of Guatemala. In doing so, he hoped to free himself from the state of mental paralysis in which he felt trapped since the suicide of his twin brother.

He looked through his seat window and realized the Boeing had just begun its descent to Guatemala City Airport. They were flying over the highest peaks of the Sierra Madre. The mountain range appeared to him like the crested back of a giant stegosaurus. In that vision, Lake Atitlan represented the jade green eye of the dinosaur following the plane's descent path. The columns of white smoke spewed by active volcanoes added to the sensation of going back in time in a vast prehistoric landscape.

The Mission

Guatemala City Airport

May 1979

In a line of mostly Ladinos, mixed-race descendants of Spanish conquerors, and a few Mayan adults, Paul was the only white man waiting to get through immigration and Guatemalan entry controls at La Aurora International Airport. Of medium height and thickset, with thinning blond hair, a well-lined face, and tanned skin from working in the open air and near the sea, he looked more like a young farmer than an intellectual who had completed a master's degree in sociology.

On his right, a Guatemalan soldier, looking impassive, with a machine gun in his hands, was leaning against a wall under a sign saying *"Bienvenido a Guatemala."* With inspections at the point of entry proceeding rather slowly, Paul began daydreaming, recalling the last moments spent with his family when leaving the family farm near the town of Camden, Maine. He remembered how tense he was before bidding farewell, especially to his mother.

While his father helped him to push his traveling trunk in the back of their pick-up truck and secure it with ropes, his mother and sisters waited silently by the passenger side cab.

Paul had taken one last look at their farmland. It was gently sloping down to the sea behind the barn. Holstein cows were scattered within a fenced field on the other side of the country road going past the farm. In the distance, a small stream ran down a low hill and meandered through the field. He could almost smell the unmistakable odor of freshly mown hay mixed with the salty air carried by a very light easterly breeze.

Paul's father got in the cab and started the engine, thus signaling departure. Paul walked towards his mother to embrace her. Her eyes were bleary and swollen from having shed too many tears and having slept very little. He kissed her on the cheeks.

"Where is Louise?" she asked in a quavering voice.

"She's not coming. We said goodbye yesterday. She told me she did not want to add to our sorrow."

She smiled sadly and gently stroked his face.

"Be careful, and don't forget to write to us."

"Mom don't worry, I'm not leaving forever. It's just a two-year contract. I'll probably be back a few times before then."

Then he had hugged his younger sisters and kissed them. The youngest couldn't stop crying, and when he turned to get into the pickup, he couldn't stop a tear from slowly running down his cheek.

They drove up to a little bridge spanning the small stream, crossed it, and continued their way on the road leading to Camden.

After a while, his father looked appealingly to Paul and said, "People are talking you know."

"What do they say?"

"I heard things like 'Paul is a man with a big heart, but when he decided to leave for Guatemala, I found it a bit strange. He leaves his fiancée, Louise, a well-paid job, his family, his friends, and his native land he so much loves. I thought I knew him well, but even considering what happened to his family, there's a link I don't see."

"And you dad, what do you say?"

"It's hard for me to accept the fact that you are going away, but I think I understand why you do this. You had to find a way to get you out of the months of lethargy you were trapped in since your brother's death. You're going to help people in need. I'm proud of you, son. But two years..."

As they were approaching the entrance of the cemetery, Paul's dad asked, "Do you still want to make a stop?"

"Please."

They left the main road and turned onto the gravel path running between rows of gravestones guarded by large silver maples. The moving reflections of their long branches on the windshield gave the impression of a strange ghostly dance.

After a long silence, Paul's father began to talk about his wife.

"When your mother learned what you had decided to do, she cried all night, lamenting and saying, 'I have just lost a son and I'm afraid I will never see my dear Paul again.' When I woke up in the morning, she was sitting in her armchair with her rosary beads interlaced around her fingers. Before I could speak, she said, 'I understand that it was a call from God. It must be.'"

Not wanting to dwell on that sad topic, Paul had looked at his father and said, "I don't know if you have noticed, but I haven't come here since the funeral. I think I'll have a hard time finding Francis's grave."

"That's what I thought. We are almost there."

They both had then paid more attention to the tombstones scrolling in front of them. A few seconds later, his father stopped and pointed to a group of headstones.

"There he is, the one with the fly fisherman carved on it."

"I remember how much I welcomed the idea. The three of us have enjoyed so many good times together going out fishing."

At this memory, Paul had felt a sudden and strong emotion. He had opened the door to get out, but had stopped in mid-stride, leaving it partially open. He bowed his head a moment, trying to keep his self-control, and then started to reveal why he had not come before.

"Shortly after the burial, I began to feel his presence around me, and most of the time it happened just before falling asleep. As you know, sometimes we felt that we could read each other's mind, as if we were able to communicate via telepathy. So, I thought Francis was trying to contact me, and it scared the hell out of me. I begged him to let me be, using the excuse that I was not ready for this. That's why I did not want to get close to his body. I felt guilty because I thought I was letting him down. Today I understand that my fears were mostly the result of my imagination, but the pain I felt was real, like an amputee's pain. I could not accept the idea he's gone forever."

"How could you endure such pain without talking to me or your mother?"

"I was living in a daze, trapped in a glass box. I was ashamed and the experience left me feeling bruised for a long time. But now that I have freed myself from this perverse brain mechanism, I am ready to say adieu to Francis."

"Okay, fine. I'll wait for you in the pick-up."

Paul got out and started to walk through the first row of

tombstones. As soon as he was able to read the name of his twin brother, he could no longer feel his legs. He continued moving forward with the impression of floating above the ground, his eyes fixed on the engraved name: Francis Desilets.

Some shoving and shouting abruptly brought him back to the airport. On the other side of the check-in counter for incoming passengers, two armed customs officers were ordering a couple of Mayas to open their suitcases on a table. Once the suitcases were opened, their owners were brutally pushed away. Then the customs officers turned the suitcases over and began checking their contents before setting them aside in a messy pile. They openly showed their disgust while handling the couple's belongings. The smallest gestures of the middle-aged couple were under constant scrutiny by two policemen, and so they hardly dared to move. They seemed resigned to be sent directly before a firing squad.

While Paul watched the whole scene in disbelief and shock, he heard someone shouting commandingly. He looked at the soldier still leaning under the welcome sign. The man signaled him with his automatic rifle to move forward. Paul then realized that the waiting line had shortened. In fact, he had moved forward automatically while reliving the last moments before his departure, and he was next in line.

Still a little shaken, Paul proceeded to the point of entry and gave his passport, including his work visa, to the immigration officer who stood behind a protective glass. The eyes of the officer moved rapidly while reading the information on the document, until they stopped on the work visa. Keeping his eyes on the visa stamp, the officer started to ask the usual questions.

"How much time do you intend to stay in Guatemala?"

"I have signed a two-year contract."

The officer took a quick glance at Paul's face, verified against his passport photograph, and then continued to talk without looking up.

"Your name?"

"Paul Desilets."

"What is the name of the company you work for?"

"I work as a humanitarian aid worker for a Foreign Mission Society."

Hearing the last words, the officer tensed up and started to use a threatening tone.

"Do you have a formal authorization?"

Paul took out an envelope from his jacket pocket and handed it to the officer.

"Here's a letter from the Bishop of Quetzaltenango, Monsignor Oscar Urizar. I believe it's also signed by the military commander of the region where I am assigned."

The officer carefully examined the contents of the letter. When finished, he abruptly pushed back the letter and passport through the opening, looking at Paul with contempt. Paul promptly recovered his papers.

"*Pase*", the officer finally said in a low voice tinged with disgust.

Feeling uncomfortable, Paul moved away before looking back to see the contempt on the face of the officer turning into a smirk.

Father Callaghan

Paul entered the arrivals hall, stopped after a few steps and began to scan the boisterous crowd coming and going in the passenger terminal, looking for the person who was supposed to have come to greet him. A porter was following closely behind him, pushing a luggage cart carrying his large trunk. Seeing that nobody was there to meet him, Paul asked the porter to wait inside while he would go look outside the terminal.

When he emerged into the glaring sunlight, he had to raise his right hand to shade his eyes to get a good look at the white van pulling up in front of him. As he got out of the vehicle, Father Callaghan appeared to him in an aura of light. He was a tall, grizzled man with the marked face of someone who had been around for a while. He welcomed Paul with a big warm smile.

"Paul Desilets? John Callaghan! Welcome into the very heart of the world of the origin, as the Mayas say... It's a pleasure to meet you, and I apologize for coming in late. I had to borrow the minivan from a Jesuit colleague working in San Juan, who himself was late."

"I've just arrived Father Callaghan."

"Please, just call me John."

They enthusiastically shook hands. Paul felt relieved to

finally be welcomed in a warm spirit of friendship and hospitality in Guatemala. But soon a soldier walked toward them. He pointed his sub-machine gun at the minivan and commanded them to leave.

"*Prohibido estacionar aquí!*"

Father Callaghan put his hand out in peace.

"*Si, si, hermano. Nos vamos...*"

The soldier did not answer to that but again pointed his gun in a way that told them they better move quickly.

While Father Callaghan was dealing with the soldier, Paul looked for his porter, who had awaited stoically inside the hall. He waved him out and asked him to bring the trunk to the back of the minivan.

After having given a bribe to the young and impatient soldier, the priest opened the back doors of the minivan and hopped into it to make some room by moving an old Jawa motorcycle, encrusted with earth and partly rusted, that was lying on the side. Then he helped Paul slide the trunk beside the motorcycle. Paul paid the porter and joined Father Callaghan in the cab of the van, and they drove off. The young soldier watched them until they disappeared from his sight.

They left the city on the Pan-American Highway, which runs north-south through the heart of the Mayan country in the rural highlands of Guatemala. They quickly climbed the ascending road and Paul saw the capital gradually disappear in his rearview mirror.

In the van, Father Callaghan remained silent for a while, as if to give his passenger the opportunity to appreciate the mountainous landscape of the Mayan territory with its typical villages surrounded by *milpas*, those small squares of land cultivated on mountainsides, visible at various distances and heights on both sides of the road. It was the end of the dry season and the corn had recently been harvested, giving the impression that the mountains were covered with huge patchwork of pale-yellow woven patterns.

At the foot of the hills, women in traditional blouses and skirts were washing clothes in small streams; behind them, brightly colored clothes were sun drying on the ground. Sometimes they passed small groups of women walking against the traffic, chatting nonchalantly, while carrying large baskets full of washed or dried clothes on their head. The contrast with the tension Paul had felt in the airport terminal was striking. These people seemed perfectly at ease in their natural environment.

Seeing that Paul looked more relaxed, that he had the time to decompress after the shock of the arrival in the so called "New World," Callaghan started to give a presentation on the situation.

"I'm sure you'd been briefed before coming here and you must have a pretty good understanding of the current situation in Guatemala but let me give you my take on it."

Surprised to hear Callaghan's voice, Paul glanced at him, hesitating between curiosity and fear of having to listen to a didactic lecture.

Noticing the apprehension in Paul's eyes, Callaghan added, "Sorry, but I have to do this. I'll try to make it short and sweet." He winked at Paul and began his lecture while looking back at the road they drove on. Paul turned to look again at the scenery through the side window while listening to the words of the priest.

"The Maya make up more than 75% of the population of

this mountainous region of Guatemala, as they do in Chiapas, Mexico. For these people, diversification of activities is the golden rule of survival. Their economy is based on subsistence agriculture with crops of corn, beans, squash, and potatoes grown on small plots of land, complemented by handicrafts made of vegetable fibers, woven products, and wood carvings, and by occasional or professional trade. The weekly markets are traditional poles of activity, some of them drawing a large clientele to smaller villages. In addition, more than three hundred thousand seasonal workers, men, women, and children, go to the plantations of the Pacific coast where the crops require a large workforce...

... The Mayas and Aztecs were here long before us, and the Mayan ancestors created a very advanced civilization well before the Christian era. At the end of the Middle Ages, they were still more advanced than the Westerners in many aspects. Thus, at the time of the conquest of the New World, although the Mayan civilization had begun its fall a few centuries earlier, it was our own ancestors who were considered barbarians by the Mayas. So, their roots are very deep. Today, more than two million Mayas live in this ancestral land...

... Although most of the businesses, services and municipal governments are owned and operated by German and Spanish descendants in the larger cities such as Huehuetenango or Quetzaltenango, the rural areas, villages, and outskirts of the cities are almost exclusively Maya. These underdeveloped regions have given rise to a dynamic and mobile population that travels on pilgrimages or to traditional markets. That is why you still see some Natives walking on the paths, mountain trails and the roads that cross their territory, but hardly on the streets of the major cities of Guatemala."

As he listened to the priest, Paul began to pay more attention to the men who were climbing mountain trails that became steeper and steeper as they moved deeper into Mayan territory. Father Callaghan explained that these men, moving like ants on huge ant hills, carried huge bundles of wood, bags of corn or dried beans on their backs that could well weigh more than a hundred pounds, all held together by a simple leather strap fastened around the head. They were moving silently, leaning forward as if they were constantly overburdened by a sustained effort, even when they were not carrying a load.

"You can see that these direct descendants have literally clung to the slightest plot of cropland."

Paul was struck by the strength and endurance of these men, acting as their ancestors probably had thousands of years before.

"You take me on a journey through time."

"I had the same impression when I first came here," Father Callaghan said. "We live on the same planet, but here we feel we are entering into an unknown world. Another revealing key characteristic of the mentality of the Mayan people is that since the Spanish Conquest, which took place nearly 500 years ago, the word 'conquest' was never translated or introduced into the various Mayan languages; rather, it is referred to as occupied territory."

At a bend in the road, the van passed by a machine gun nest lurking behind a wall of sandbags. Troubled by this sign of a military presence, Paul looked at Callaghan.

"Don't worry! It's just a staging to remind the Mayas that they have been conquered. The Natives act like it's part of the scenery. Why do you think we set up military bases not too far from the Native American reserves in Canada and the United

States? The main difference is that here the display of power seems... more macho."

It occurred to Paul that the priest had probably staged his presentation, or perhaps he had done it before, because most of his highlights corresponded to the landscape elements scrolling before their eyes.

Immediately after the bend, the road became steeper, and the van was rapidly catching up with a so-called 'chicken bus' (a modified and colorfully decorated school bus commonly used to transport goods and people between communities in different Latin American countries). With its roof covered with secured luggage, the bus struggled up the long climb to a high pass, belching out large clouds of black smoke.

At its highest point, the road had been carved out of a mountain peak and was lined with high rock walls on which two large signs had been screwed. The one on the left said "*No critiquemos a Guatemala*" and the other "*Trabajemos no critiquemos.*" Father Callaghan read them aloud before translating them to Paul as follows: "In Guatemala, we don't criticize" and "Let's work and not criticize."

Then, after glancing at his passenger, he added with a derisive smile, "Doesn't that remind you of something?"

Having no idea, Paul shook his head.

"At the entrance to the Auschwitz-Birkenau concentration camp, the Nazis posted the inscription '*Arbeit macht frei*' which could be translated as 'Work makes you free'."

Paul nodded, showing that he understood the hint very well.

The bus they had approached on the way up was now rapidly moving away on the downhill side of the pass they had just crossed. The clouds of black smoke that escaped from it now seemed to swirl happily and mischievously above the minivan.

At the bottom of the hill, they turned right onto a new ascending road, a side road that was paved but in poor condition, its surface cracked and bumpy. From then on, the landscape began to close in around them. The terrain became generally more rugged, with mountain peaks too high to be seen from the van. Then the road narrowed further and began to snake like a riverbed winding its way through a steep valley.

After several minutes of driving along that long winding road, the landscape suddenly unfolded before them, revealing wider valleys surrounded by lower hills. This time they turned left onto a dirt road that ran parallel to the blue mountains of the *Sierra de los Cuchumatanes*, visible in the distance. Surprisingly, this road proved to be much more drivable than the last paved one. Father Callaghan announced that they were entering the Concepción area. Then he seemed to suddenly remember something.

"Tell me Paul, have you ever ridden a motorcycle?"

"I don't know if that qualifies, but on my parents' farm we used to ride a dirt bike to get the cows in the field."

"Good, good! Because you see, the bike in the back of the van needs a new clutch pedal. The Jesuits in San Juan were kind enough to give it to us, but we have to fix it ourselves, and I know nothing about mechanics."

"I don't know much about that either, but I'm willing to try and do my best to fix it."

"I would really appreciate it. When I asked the Mission Society to provide me with a van like this one, I was told that I had to make do with my emoluments. I sometimes think I should have chosen to become a Jesuit priest. I don't know how they do it, but it looks like they always get what they need."

Then seeing the puzzled look of his fellow traveler, he went on, saying, "Sorry it was an inside... Well, listen carefully, you'll understand... Four Catholic monks are gathered in a room to discuss theological issues. The discussion is well underway when the power goes out. The Franciscan monk kneels and asks the Lord to bring back the light. The Benedictine monk recites his breviary that he knows by heart, convinced that it will get him into the Lord's favors. The Dominican monk launches into a rhetorical statement about light and darkness in our world. Suddenly, the lights come back on and the three of them are worried because the Jesuit monk has disappeared. When he reappears a few moments later, they ask where he has been.

"Ho," replies the Jesuit monk, "I just went to change the fuses."

"I see where you're going with this. More pragmatic, more down-to-earth," Paul said, laughing heartily.

The Village of Concepción

Concepción looked like a fairytale village. From a distance, it took the shape of a crescent moon nestled at the foot of a hill on its east side. The road Father Callaghan took ran along the western edge of the village and was bordered by small woods and thickets on the opposite side, at the foot of gently rounded hills, carpeted with small, cultivated fields and dotted with a few stands of deciduous trees. It was a dreamy, rounded landscape that enchanted Paul.

As they approached the village, the surrounding hills seemed to roll away from them. In the middle of this shifting setting, Paul could spot the white domed roof of the village church, glowing under the sun. After driving along the cemetery located on the northwest end of the village, they turned left to get on the main street that led to the public square. Small Spanish-style houses with yellow, pink, blue or white adobe walls and tile roofs lined the unpaved streets.

The few people they met on the main street greeted Father Callaghan warmly. A small group of peasants returning from the fields, machetes in hand, emerged from a side street. Their looks and smiles clearly expressed their affection and goodwill toward the priest as they recognized him. Paul felt even more like he was entering a new world. The way these people looked at them was guileless and full of kindness.

A bit further along the main street, a young woman in traditional costume was standing on her porch with a baby harnessed to her back. She looked up at the approaching van, frowning, wondering who these people were, but as the van passed by, she recognized Father Callaghan, who called out her name. She greeted him with a bright smile. But when she saw Paul's head come out of the passenger window to look at her, she froze, her hand hanging in the air. She eventually gave him a timid smile.

When reaching the town square, they went round it to the right, then right again along the north wall of the church until they finally took left onto the street leading to the southern exit of the village. They passed slowly in front of the church forecourt, then entered the large dirt courtyard next to it, and stopped in front of the large porch that spanned the width of the rectory.

Father Callaghan turned to Paul and said, "There you go! This building serves as a presbytery. I live in a three-room apartment on the left side. On the right side, there are three large rooms and a common bathroom with shower, for our rare visitors. Right now, there's no one there, so you can choose."

As they got out of the van, a Mayan adult in his thirties, short, stocky and pudgy like the surrounding landscape came out of the church through a side door and walked towards them with smiling eyes.

"Ah! It's José!" the priest announced enthusiastically. And then in a low voice, "He's the village teacher and a member of the municipal council. He probably wants to welcome you."

"*Buenas tardes*, Padre John."

"*Hola José, como estas? Como esta Anna?*"

"*Está bien, tres meses hasta que llegue el bebé* [She is doing fine, three more months until the baby arrives]."

Father Callaghan smiled at this encouraging news, and then turning to Paul, "Paul, I'd like you to meet José Alguilar, one of our very good friends. (Then to José) Paul is an aid worker who's coming to work with us."

José bowed and extended his hand to Paul who happily accepted it.

"I am delighted to meet you, Paul. (Then turning to the priest) With your permission, I must return home. (Then to Paul again) See you soon!"

As the two missionaries watched him walk away, Father Callaghan said, "José is someone you get to know. He's highly respected in the area."

"I'm surprised he speaks our language so well."

"Indeed, it's rather rare considering that a substantial number of Natives don't even speak Spanish, especially in remote regions. The basic language of our parishioners is the *Mam* dialect, but most of them can speak Spanish, and some speak broken English ... José's keen intelligence drew the attention of some Franciscan brothers who decided to educate him before sending him to the University of Quetzaltenango where he became friends with an English teacher," Callaghan explained while waving to José who was doing the same before disappearing into the street.

Then returning to Paul, "But you must be exhausted. Let's go choose your room. You still have time to rest before supper. The food is simple, but you will see that Graciela, my housekeeper, is a good cook."

"I'll try to follow your advice Father John. It's true that I'm a little shaky, and I have a slight headache. A little nap can only do me good."

"Come on Paul, please, it's John! We're going to be working together for the next two years, and I'd rather not have that kind of barrier between us.

Paul looked down and said, "Sorry, Father... um... John."

"Don't worry. You'll get used to it soon enough," the priest encouraged him, patting Paul on the shoulder.

Paul opted for a small room modestly furnished with a folding bed, a chamber pot, an open wardrobe with few hangers, a desk with drawers on both sides, which could be used to store clothes, an empty basin on a small wooden nightstand and a hardwood chair. The only decoration was a crucifix hanging on the wall above the headboard.

Sweating and breathing hard, the two missionaries entered the room carrying Paul's heavy trunk. They placed it on the floor next to the bed and took their time to catch their breath, the priest sitting on the bed, and Paul on the only chair.

"You chose well. It's sober but welcoming," Father Callaghan finally said, still panting. He pointed to the only window which looked out over the eastern part of the village, and added, "You can enjoy the evening breeze. (Then, pointing to the basin) Graciela will come and fill the vase with fresh water and empty the chamber pot in the afternoon, if not already done... The water pump is at the end of the corridor."

"It's perfect!"

"Good. I'll leave you alone now. Don't forget supper, at seven... Get some rest," Callaghan added as he stood up. He left the room with a smile of contentment on his face.

Once the door was closed, Paul left his seat to open his trunk. He took out a large brown envelope from which he removed three photos and pinned them to the wall above the desk: a photo of his mother and father proudly posing in front of the family farm, another showing Paul with his two sisters and his brother Francis, and finally a photo of his fiancée. He kept his eyes fixed on the latter for a moment.

Sounds from outside caught his attention. He went to his window and looked out at the few houses on the only two streets at the foot of the hill bordering the village to the east. He smiled as he recognized the cries of children playing. He glanced at his open trunk, hesitated, and decided to lie down on his bed. He closed his eyes and let himself be lulled by the laughter and the bursts of voices that slowly faded away.

Work Assignment

The small three-room apartment in which Father Callaghan stayed included a private bathroom, a large space divided into a living and dining area, the kitchen and the bedroom.

At 7:30 p.m., Paul, who had changed and shaved, was sitting with Father Callaghan at the priest's table. They watched as Graciela, the plump old Mayan housekeeper, came out of the kitchen with a tray full of corn tortillas and small bowls containing pieces of chicken, rice, and black beans coated with a brown sauce, which she brought to their table.

Immediately after Graciela returned to her kitchen, Father Callaghan hurried to fetch a bottle of red wine and two small glasses from a small cupboard. Paul was amused by the nervous glances the priest gave to the kitchen during the operation.

As soon as he came back to the table, the latter proudly exhibited a corkscrew that he kept in a shirt pocket, and while opening the bottle, he said in a low voice, "It's a gift my sister gave me during her latest visit."

He was finishing removing the cork when he gave a last glance at the kitchen. Graciela was staring at him, fists on hips and a grim look on her face. Caught in the act, Callaghan tried to justify himself in Spanish: "Come on, Graciela! Don't you think we should welcome our guest with all due respect?"

"In any case I'm not the one who will be sick," Graciela retorted curtly, before disappearing in the kitchen again.

Paul smiled at the thought that they made an odd couple.

"Well, we can say that she takes good care of you."

"Bah! Sometimes she does too much, but I'm sure glad to have her with me," Father Callaghan said with a wink. Then he hurriedly poured the wine into their glasses until they were almost full to the brim, and raised his own.

"I propose a toast to the Mission Society. Blessed be it for sending you here."

They toasted and drank, Paul only dipping his lips, aware that he might be tested, while Father Callaghan took a big swig that seemed to cheer him up. His eyes brightened.

"As you may know, when the Mission Society sent its first contingent of priests and missionaries to Central America in the early 1950s, their work was generally to fight communism, Protestantism and concubinage.... I think that our current work more adequately reflects the message of compassion and love preached by Jesus... Amen!" Then raising his glass again, "To our future collaboration!"

After taking another big swig, he poured more wine into his glass and, as he was about to do the same with Paul's, he hesitated for a split second when he realized that his guest's glass was relatively untouched; he put the bottle back on the table and looked down at his plate.

"Let's eat now! We'll need all our strength to do our job."

Paul watched the priest's technique carefully. The latter used a spoon to spread the rice, chicken, and beans on a tortilla, which he then rolled up and folded over at the ends. Paul's first attempt proved less than successful, with almost half the contents falling onto his plate and the table. But the priest's indulgent smile, while eating with enthusiasm, encouraged him.

Paul's second tortilla was nearly perfect, but before he could take a bite out of it Father Callaghan spoke up again, saying, "Um! So... I assume you've been well briefed on the work you'll be doing here..."

"Oh, it was pretty general. I was told that I would help people run their cooperative and do outreach work with the youth."

"Your main task will be to set up a group of young teenagers and to prepare them for the modern world. Among other things, we intend in the medium term to organize cultural exchanges with young people from other countries. We want our youth to see what modern society looks like, and we want youth in developed countries to learn that there are other ways to live. I would also really appreciate it if you could help a young medical student from the University of Quetzaltenango open a medical clinic, here in the village. After setting it up, I would like you to do the management, schedule health consultations, ensure continuity, etc.... You can use the motorcycle as you like if you can fix it. Oh, except on Sundays. I'll need it to go and say mass in the surrounding villages. But first you must get to know the village and its people. And tomorrow you'll have a good opportunity to do that, as it will be market day in Concepción, and almost everyone from the surrounding area will come to the town square."

Paul, still holding his untouched tortilla, finally answered the priest's questioning gaze.

"It suits me just fine. I didn't come here to twiddle my thumbs."

"Perfect! Callaghan replied. You can finish your tortilla

now," he added with a disarming smile.

Understanding that the priest was ready to move on, Paul hurried to finish eating. Callaghan took the opportunity to empty his second glass, then greedily eyed the half-empty bottle. He glanced at Paul who stared down to hide his embarrassment. Resisting the temptation, Callaghan put the cork back in. He then laid his hands on the table, looked at the two armchairs at the other end of the room and said mockingly, "Let's have coffee in the living room."

"Gladly" Paul replied as he stood up.

The living room consisted of two old, worn, but comfortable upholstered armchairs on either side of a vintage coffee table with a magazine rack and a standing lamp. As soon as they were seated, Graciela came out of the kitchen with a coffee pot, two cups and plates, and milk and sugar on the same tray she had used for the meal. She placed it on the coffee table, letting both men fix their coffee, and she hastened to get the food off the table, not forgetting the bottle of wine she grabbed under the disapproving gaze of Father Callaghan.

Having tasted the coffee, Paul was pleasantly surprised with its good taste.

"Um, this coffee is excellent!"

"This type of high-quality coffee can only be found in Guatemala City. Guatemala's coffee plantations are famous all over the world, but you see, almost all the coffee produced is for export only. It's only available in a few places and at a high price. An American doctor, Charles Ramsay, who works for the NGO Doctors without Borders, gave it to me as a gift. He's the one who will supervise the implementation of the medical clinic."

With that, they both took a deep sip of coffee, then

Callaghan resumed his questioning.

"I think I've read in your documents that you have worked with young teenagers."

"Oh, very little. During a social work internship, I oversaw a group of young offenders who didn't give a damn. I admit that it hasn't been much of a success."

"What happened?"

"They were rabid, like stray dogs that have been kicked in the ribs and slapped in the back of the head too many times. You'd reach out your hand, they'd bite it. I couldn't get them to trust me."

"Did they bite you?" Callaghan cut him off mockingly.

"Worse! Some of them even stole my car and wrecked it in an accident. Fortunately, no one was seriously hurt."

"Well, you'll enjoy working with the kids here even more. You'll be glad to see a change in thinking and attitudes. The pitfalls will be of a different order. You see, in Guatemala, a group of people which are part of an association like a Youth Center could be suspected of being tinted with left-wing sympathies. We have to be very careful about what we say or do in this country."

At this point, Callaghan paused to make sure Paul was taking his words seriously. Then, in a lighter tone, he added, "But since we are acting under the authority of the Church, I think our young people should be protected from the kind of paranoia that plagues all fascist governments. Still, you'll have to be careful."

Paul nodded, looking serious, and the priest went on, "Good! While we are on this, I took the liberty of inviting a few teenagers to come and meet you on Monday evening, the day after tomorrow; nothing formal, just a question of breaking the ice and getting to know each other. I hope it suits you."

"That's okay with me. The sooner's the better, in my view."

"You seem to be quite an easy-going person."

"I'm just trying to be a good Catholic," Paul replied with a smile. "And I think we shall give the nuns credit for that."

"You could say we owe them a lot of credit," added Father Callaghan, chuckling. "I remember my first-grade teacher, Sister Mary of the Angels... She thought it was the devil that made me confuse letters b and d. She talked about it with the priest who was assigned to our school, and he turned out to be much more astute. He ended up telling the good sister and my parents that I was simply mentally retarded."

That made them laugh heartily.

Market Day

The next day, the public square was transformed into a marketplace crowded with people from the village and the surrounding area. The traditional Mayan costumes were blooming in a jungle of bright colors.

People came to sell or buy a variety of foods, including melons, potatoes, garlic, peppers, pigs, and chickens; all kinds of hardware, including watches, combs, mirrors, tin cups, and other cheap metal objects; and handicrafts such as the 'huipil', a kind of woolen blouse that fell wide at the waist. All those products were displayed in market stalls mounted on wooden frames.

The Mayas that Father Callaghan and Paul encountered along the way to and in the marketplace greeted them by saying *"Buenas días"* with modulated voices.

As the priest had stopped to chat with a woman carrying her baby in a backpack, Paul let himself get caught up in browsing through the stalls. He finally lingered in front of a leather shop, attracted by a hand-sewn saddle hanging from a trestle. The owner greeted him with a big smile,

"Buenos días señor". He pointed at the saddle. "You like this saddle?"

"It's very beautiful."

"If you want it, I make special price for you."

"I'd love to buy one of these, but I have to find a horse first," Paul said as he began to walk away.

That made the saddler laugh.

"Yes, yes, first a horse and then a saddle!" the man replied with a wave.

In the early afternoon, on the same day, Paul had the crazy idea of exploring alone the neighboring countryside that the local people called Tuipoch. He wore his Panama-style straw hat, the crown of which was decorated with a red ribbon with a green polka dot pattern. He walked from the rectory to the south end of the village, where the street forked left, leading to the top of the hill overlooking the village. Paul struggled to climb the rounded slope, and he had to stop a few times to catch his breath.

On his way up, he encountered a group of women going to the marketplace with baskets on their heads and young children clinging to their skirts. They did not seem too surprised to see him, being rather amused by his presence. He thought that the news of his arrival had spread quickly. Some of the children, fascinated by the stranger, called out, "*Hey Gringo, Gringo!*" But when Paul looked up at them, they quickly hid behind their mothers' skirts, giggling with excitement. He lifted his hat to greet the ladies and took the opportunity to ask for directions. While asking, he winked at the children, who showed their faces and stared at him with wide eyes.

At first, the women did not seem to understand his Spanish, but upon hearing the word Tuipoch, one of them pointed to the top of the hill. Paul lifted his hat again and thanked them.

"*Muchas gracias, señoras!*"

Then, looking up the hill, he had the impression that the road ahead went up indefinitely to the sky. He felt a bit downhearted. To encourage himself, he set a large boulder halfway up the road as an intermediate target. Once reaching it, he sat on the flat stone and looked down. The children were still turning to look at the intriguing *gringo*. He waved at them, and they waved back. The scenery was spectacular. At the sight of this magnificent hilly landscape, seeming to unfold more deeply before him than when he arrived in the village, he felt a slight dizziness.

Meeting José and his Family

When he finally reached the top of the hill, Paul discovered the heights of the Tuipoch hamlet, set on an expanse of semi-arid land stretching for some distance and descending gently eastward to the foot of another steeper hill. On his left, the Cuchumatanes mountain range was running diagonally northeast in the far distance. On his right, a path led to a group of small houses built on a more fertile type of soil, allowing the cultivation of small gardens.

Not far from where he stood, Paul recognized José Mejia Alguilar. He and a few others were busy cutting out blocks of earth from a large pit. Several of them were already piled up all around, put to dry in the sun and become adobe bricks, of which most of the walls of the hamlet's houses were made. Two women, one quite young and visibly pregnant, and an elder, carrying baskets on their heads, were joining the workers. Coming out of the pit to meet them, José was intrigued by the puzzled looks of the two women who were staring at something behind him. He turned to the road leading to the village and saw Paul approaching and waving. José invited him to join.

"*Buenos días*, Paul. You came alone?"

Still out of breath, Paul nodded. Not far from them, a few young girls doing laundry in a concrete basin were glancing at them inquisitively.

"But you are breathless!" José said, while shaking hands with him.

"It's probably the altitude," Paul replied, still gasping a little. "I just wanted to visit the surroundings and see some croplands."

"Unfortunately, it's not the right season to see the crops."

"I know, but I grew up on a farm and (pointing to the landscape all around) it reminds me of where I come from."

José turned to the pregnant young woman, who was laying out food on a tablecloth spread on the ground.

"My mother and my wife, Anna, have just arrived and we are about to take a snack before they go down to the market... Would you like to join us for a bite?"

"I'm really in no condition to refuse. I'm starving, so I gladly accept."

José, in a friendly gesture, took Paul's elbow and led him to the women.

"Come, let me introduce you... Paul, I would like you to meet my mother, Christina, and my wife, Anna."

"*Encantado de conocerle* [Nice to meet you]," Paul managed to say in Spanish.

José looked at the women and said in *Mam*, their Mayan dialect, "This is Paul Desilets, the new missionary who comes to help Father Callaghan."

The two women greeted Paul with a slight bow. Paul returned the favor by doing the same.

In trying to pronounce Paul's name, Anna made her stepmother laugh when she said what sounded like, "*Padre Pooul?*"

Smiling, José corrected her.

"Paul is not a priest, but a layman like us, and he's familiar with the work on the land."

Anna smiled back and asked in Spanish, "Is he going to help us work in the fields?"

"No, he won't. I don't think so," José replied, while turning to Paul.

Having understood what this was all about, Paul spoke up.

"This is not why I was hired, but I admit I'm curious about your working methods, and I hope to be able to help out from time to time," he managed to explain in Spanish to Anna.

While the men continued to talk among themselves, Anna and her mother-in-law prepared them tortillas with meat and vegetable. Once the meal was ready, they all started to eat. Paul took his first bite and his eyes lit up.

"Ladies, it's delicious. Just for that, it was well worth the effort to go all the way up here." Then remembering that José's mother could not understand him, he smiled and held up his right thumb saying, "*Muy, muy sabroso!*"

After a few more bites of food, he nodded at a small cultivated plot located behind a mud brick house and asked José, "What do you grow on these small plots of land?"

"Mostly corn, beans and squash, the 'three sisters', as our ancestors called them."

"Three different crops in such a small area; the soil must be very fertile?"

José smiled, turned to his mother, who was finishing eating, and said in *Mam*, "Paul thinks the land is very fertile because we grow three crops."

"Tell him that the land is good, but it gets tired easily, just like an old woman like me," his mother replied.

José and the two women laughed.

"My mother says that the soil is good for us, but that we

must ask too much of it, because it depletes quickly." Then, more seriously, "Since fresh water is a scarcer resource in our region, we must practice crop rotation, which, as you probably know, helps to retain nutrients in the soil... So here we use the mixed agricultural technique of complementary crops, called the three sisters, representing the three main crops traditionally grown by the Central American Natives: squash, corn, and beans. This combination has proven to be the most beneficial for our land, the one that ensures the best productivity."

The two women picked up the snack leftovers and put baskets on their heads.

Anna walked up to José and said in *Mam*, "Tell him he may come to our home."

José, laying his hands on Anna's belly, "Be careful! Take your time!"

"Will you stop worrying, I already told you that she and the baby are doing great," his mother retorted. Then she waved to Paul and the two women set off for the village. The men watched them walk away for a moment before Paul turned to José saying, "She looks good."

"I confess to being a little concerned. The death rate at birth is quite high in our population. I know, however, that this happens especially in the poorest regions and that our midwife is experienced and very efficient. Everyone tells me that I worry unnecessarily, but I can't help it."

"My mother told me that my dad had been sick for weeks before I was born, while she herself was doing fine. I'm sorry, José, but I think you are showing symptoms of a phantom pregnancy," Paul teased him.

José laughed and showed his belly, protesting, "No, no,

no!"

Having managed to wring a smile out of José, Paul became serious again and asked, looking a little embarrassed, "I'd like to learn your dialect and be able to talk with your people. Would you accept to teach it to me?"

Jose looked at him for a moment, as if gauging him, then nodded.

"When do you want to start?"

"Whenever you want."

After a bit of thought, José pointed a finger toward the footpath that joined the road linking Tuipoch with Concepción. With his finger, he pointed along the path to the sixth house, "My house is the sixth one along that path, the one partly hidden by trees. Come by at 8:00 p.m. Wednesday evening, if you can."

"Great! Thanks José. I'll be there. I hope it won't be too boring for you and Anna."

"It might be fun and rather embarrassing for you," José retorted.

"All right then! I'll leave you to your work. I have to fix Father John's bike; it will be much easier to come up here if I succeed."

The Repair

Later that day, Father Callaghan was returning from the town square when he heard metal components clanking together from the rectory yard. He decided to have a look. There he found Paul crouched beside the motorcycle, finishing tightening the clutch pedal.

"So? Will it run again?" he asked.

"Want to try it?" Paul offered.

"If you don't mind, I'd rather let you have the pleasure," the priest replied wincing.

Paul got on the bike and pushed the clutch pedal hard. On the third attempt, the engine screamed, and a stinky black cloud came out of the exhaust pipes. Father Callaghan started coughing and took out a handkerchief to cover his mouth and nose. Paul engaged first gear and the motorcycle leaped forward. He braked almost immediately and returned to neutral.

"Bravo!" Callaghan exclaimed with a round of applause.

With great pride, Paul took a bow and invited the priest to mount the beast. Callaghan walked slowly to the machine, looking at it apprehensively. He finally got on it, glancing anxiously at Paul.

"Take it easy! Open the throttle a little and release the clutch slowly."

The priest did the sign of the cross before revving the engine for a few seconds. He put it in first gear and slowly began to zigzag around the yard in rough figure eights, with Paul running behind, in the hope of grasping the bike and its rider before they fell. Then, seeing a smile of excitement appear on the priest's face, he let him go. The eights were almost perfect.

A Mayan ritual

Although he felt tired after his escape to Tuipoch, Paul did not dare refuse when Father Callaghan invited him to accompany him to the hill facing the church after supper. The priest had insisted, saying there was something special he wanted to show him. And Paul had to stop several times during the climb to catch his breath.

Once at the top, he wanted to take time to recuperate while admiring the panoramic view they had on the village, but Father Callaghan, recovering faster and anxious to arrive at their destination at the right time, left immediately for the opposite side. Captivated by the orange hues that draped the landscape before him as the sun descended over the western hills, Paul barely heard Callaghan's voice calling from the other side. The priest was pointing to plumes of black smoke that had begun to rise from a spot at the bottom of the next hill.

"Hurry up! They have already started."

Paul finally got the message and joined the priest. In the distance, a group of men, barely visible through the smoke, had started a brush fire between the hills.

"What's happening?"

"It comes from Luis Ortega's field. They set fire to the bushes to prepare the soil for sowing. Come! You are about to attend a Mayan ceremony," Callaghan explained.

Standing in front of the fire, an old shaman, wearing a sort of green stole embroidered with stylized orange zoomorphic designs on a white shirt, and his apprentice, turning out to be José, were tossing cans filled with copal to burn as incense.

Paul and Father Callaghan joined the small group of peasants attending the ritual. Paul's eyes were riveted on José. He was amazed to see an educated man like him acting in such a way. Suddenly, the Mayan priest stretched his arms skyward, hands opened, palms upward, and began chanting an old litany. Father Callaghan pointed to the old man and explained in a low voice that his name was Manuel and that he was the local shaman.

"He sings a prayerful chant to apologize for the wounds they are about to inflict to Mother Earth. It goes like this:

'Oh God, Father, Mother, Huitz-Hok the sacred, Lord of the hills and valleys, Lord of the forest, please be patient. I do as always that was done. Now I am presenting my offering to you, so that you may know that I am going against your will and that you may suffer from that. I will hurt you; I will plough you to feed my family; and I pray that not a single wild beast follows my footsteps, that not a single viper, scorpion, or hornet inadvertently attacks me. I pray that not a single tree inadvertently comes falling on me, nor the axe nor the machete inadvertently cuts my skin. With all my soul, I will plough you...'"

Exhausted after a long day of exploration and fascinated by this vision of a ritual aimed at reconciling human aspirations for harmony and equality with the intrinsic spirituality of nature, Paul became mesmerized by this rhythmic chant. With the dance of the brush fire reflected in his eyes, he looked alternately at the details of the whole scene: the few Mayan peasants wearing long-sleeve shirts and jeans, with straw hats on their heads; José swinging his makeshift incense burner; Manuel going along with his prayer song mingled with the voice of Father Callaghan translating the words, and the faces turning orange and red in the fire glow, and so on.

Youth Group

The next morning, twelve teenagers, ages 12 to 15, sat on two long wooden benches in the parish hall located in the rectory. They quietly waited to meet their new group leader. When Paul entered the room, they stood up. Being a little worried about their reaction, he soon realized that they were quite receptive and seemed to be well disposed toward him. Father Callaghan had been right; they seemed to be well-behaved, receptive, and interested. Paul extended his arms in an open gesture and introduced himself in Spanish.

"*Hola a todos, gracias por venir* [Hello everyone, thanks for coming]. I'm Paul, and I've been sent here to assist Father Callaghan and to help set up a *Club Juvenil*. The mission of the Youth Club would be to create a place where you can come socialize, meet other teens, organize and participate in various activities. A kind of private circle where we can talk freely about anything we want. Of course, when I say private, it means that what will be said here, would remain between us."

Paul paused for a moment to make sure they were still with him. Seeing the row of wide-open eyes fixed on him, he added, "We could do activities such as playing soccer, creating skits based on topics that interest you... whatever you want. You come up with the suggestions and we'll decide together. So, what do you say?"

"*Si señor Pooul*," some answered with enthusiasm, pronouncing the end of his name as an interrupted hoot, while others, more intimidated, simply nodded.

"Great! Okay, now, starting from my left, I'd like you to tell me your names."

Paul looked at the first youth, who stood up. As they introduced themselves, he wrote down their names in a small notebook he had pulled out of a denim bag slung over his shoulder.

"Arnoldo Zuniga Sotelo," said the first.

"Mimo Pulido Luengo," the second one.

"Lisa Ramos Romero," the third.

Then, "Luis Oc Alguilar."

"Are you related to José Alguilar?" Paul asked.

"Yes, he's my older brother."

Mireya

While Paul and the group of teenagers were getting to know each other, Father Callaghan was meeting with Mireya Perez, a beautiful, young, athletic Ladino woman with a golden complexion and large, intense brown eyes revealing her lively spirit and keen intelligence. They were sitting at the priest's dining table, reviewing the plans of the future medical clinic.

"Tell me Mireya, do you think you can get everything we will need in Quetzaltenango?"

"I'll probably have to go to the capital a few times to get some essential medical drugs. However, those drugs are either scarce or more expensive."

"We have managed to raise up to 4,000 Quetzals for the clinic."

"Oh, but that's really good! That should be enough to build a starting inventory."

Meanwhile, the young people had gathered around Paul, who had pulled out some photos and passed them around. They got excited when they saw pictures of Paul's family farm. He took a new one out.

"This is a picture of my parents' house taken during the winter. You can see that everything is covered with snow."

He passed it to one of the youngsters. Fascinated by the whiteness of the snow, some approached to look over his shoulder. The teenager who had introduced himself as Arnoldo Zuniga Sotelo came up to Paul with another photo that had just been passed to him, showing a young woman standing next to Paul with a small group of friends.

Arnoldo pointed to her and asked with a mischievous look, "Is she your lover?"

Caught off guard, and feeling on shaky ground, Paul hesitated before answering.

"Well... yes, she's my girlfriend."

"What's her name?"

"Louise," Paul answered in a slightly tremulous voice. Immediately after telling his fiancée's name, he quickly changed the subject by asking a question to another teenager who had been following the exchange.

"You, Mimo, tell me, what kind of life would you like to have in the future?"

Surprised and embarrassed, young Mimo stared at Paul, with his mouth agape.

Thinking that he had misspoken in Spanish, Paul tried another approach.

"Okay, what kind of work would you like to do later?"

"Oh well... I guess I'll work in the field," Mimo answered, still a little uncomfortable.

Paul nodded in appreciation and then turned to the boy named Jorge.

"And you, Jorge, what do you want to do when you grow up?"

Jorge took time to consider the question, and said, "Well, uh, we all are Native peasants."

Paul scratched his head, puzzled, and suddenly seemed to realize something.

"Do you all want to have your own plot of land to farm eventually?"

"*Si señor Pooul*," they all answered in chorus, nodding their heads.

"Okay, I think I get it now. So, tell me what you don't want to do later."

Jorge was the first to break the moment of silence that followed.

"I don't want to be forced to enroll in the army."

"I don't understand," Paul said, bemused. "I didn't know there was mandatory military service in Guatemala."

Jorge looked at him, tears in his eyes, unable to speak.

"About six months ago, soldiers came to the village and took Jorge and Obispo's brothers, Leon, and Juan, to forcibly enroll them. Both had just turned 15," Luis explained.

Moved and shocked by the information, Paul came near Jorge, who was keeping eyes to the floor, and stroked his head, saying, "I'm sorry; I didn't know."

Father Callaghan and Mireya were finishing the shopping list for the medical clinic when Paul came in. Noticing the worried look on his face, Father Callaghan stood up.

"Is something wrong, Paul?"

Paul glanced briefly at Mireya and said, "No, no, that's fine. It's just that I concluded the first meeting with the youth group and thought they really needed to have some fun. I find them too serious for their age. It would be good for them to play some sport. I intend to strengthen bonds with them—for example, by organizing soccer games."

"Great idea! Now come over, so I can introduce you."

Paul stepped forward and Mireya stood up. Father Callaghan walked around the table and put his right hand on the left shoulder of the young woman.

"Paul, this is Mireya Perez. She will be responsible for the proper functioning of the health clinic."

They exchanged a firm handshake and their eyes locked together for a brief moment.

"Pleased to meet you, Doctor Perez?" Paul said, smiling shyly.

"Not yet—I am actually finishing my last year of medical studies at the University of Quetzaltenango. That's partly why the clinic will open only when my course schedule allows for it, probably in the morning from 9am to 12pm, three days a week, plus Saturday afternoon. And my work here will be overseen by one of your compatriots, Dr. Charles Ramsay, from NGO Doctors Without Borders, who told me he'll try to come once a month."

With a hand gesture Father Callaghan invited Paul to sit with them.

"Before becoming a humanitarian aid worker, Paul spent some time as a social worker. But the most interesting for us is that he grew up on a farm and should be very clever with his hands. He even successfully repaired the old motorcycle I told you about, that the Jesuits gave us. He could help us with the clinic."

"Well, if he was able to repair that old, beat-up machine, I believe he can do anything," Mireya said. Then turning to Paul, "But for now, what we need most is a carpenter. Shelves and a medicine chest, among other things, must be built."

"I'm sure Paul knows how to use a hammer," Father

Callaghan added.

At these words, Paul stretched out his hands, fists clenched with both thumbs up, saying, "And I still have my two thumbs."

Mireya smiled broadly, and said, "From now on, consider yourself hired."

Secret Meeting

That night, on the Tuipoch Plateau, one could still make out the dark silhouette of the Cuchumatanes range against the starry sky and hear the distant howl of coyotes. All the houses along the hamlet's path were in darkness, with one exception: a flickering light could be seen through the kitchen window of José's house.

Inside, José and two other men, a Native, and a white man looking like the typical scholar, bearded, and wearing glasses, were sitting around a small wooden table. A candle on a small plate in the center was the only source of light in the room. Behind José, his mother, and his wife Anna, both hands softly rubbing her rounded belly, sat in semidarkness on a wooden bench against the wall. They listened to the men talk without intervening.

Sitting across from José, the white man, named David, leaned forward with an insistent look. "You understand? We're not asking people to openly show their support— just not to go down to work at the plantations on the coast until the labor dispute is settled. It's very important for all of us. Speak to your people!"

José hesitated a bit, turned and glanced worriedly at his wife, then back at the two men at the table.

"Okay, David! I'll talk to them, but I can't guarantee the

result. Most of them need that extra income. The plots are too small, and the crops are not enough to feed the families. And then we must watch out for the mayor. He doesn't want to incur the wrath of the governor of the Quetzaltenango region. But I promise. This has to change."

Routine sets in

A few weeks later, Mireya was standing in the public square, smiling contentedly as she watched two men on wooden scaffolding paint the sign 'Clínica medica' in large white letters directly onto the façade of the clinic's new building located on the northeast corner of the main street.

Inside the same building, Paul was busy putting sideboards on a shelf in what would become Mireya's office, when she arrived with a shopping bag. She set the bag down and went to examine the shelves already in place. She ran a hand over one of them and pressed it down to see how strong it was. Paul took the opportunity to pause, loosening his muscles by rolling his shoulders and stretching his neck.

Mireya praised the work done so far, saying, "It's starting to take shape. That's good work."

"We all did well. At this rate, the clinic could be up and running by next week."

"I brought tortillas. Why don't we go eat them in the square?"

Paul quickly washed his hands in a basin of water. Then went into the waiting room, where he briefly checked wall joints he had smoothed, before picking up his straw hat hanging on a peg and joined Mireya on the doorstep.

They crossed the street and stopped to look again at the

work done by the workers on the scaffolding. The sign was almost finished. The painters turned around when Paul hailed them.

"*Hola, compañeros! Es un muy buen trabajo!* [Hey, guys! This is great work]" Paul said while giving them the thumbs-up.

Delighted, the two workers also reciprocated with their thumbs up and repeated in unison, "*Si, si! Un gran trabajo!*"

Mireya and Paul waved to them, then continued to a small wooden shack used as a canteen at the west end of the public square.

"Since you brought the food, I'll pay for the drinks, offered Paul. What would you like to have?"

"Thanks. I'll have a Coke."

The snack bar was run by a plump Mayan woman. She was helped by her young daughter, who sat in a corner on a wooden stool.

Recognizing Paul, the woman greeted him. "*Buenos días señor Pooul. Como estas?*"

"*Buenos días Clara.* (Then looking at the young girl on the stool) *Hola, Nina! Como estas?*"

Surprised to be recognized by the gringo, Nina grinned shyly and looked down.

Ignoring her shyness, Paul topped that by asking, "*Dos cocas, por favor, mi bella.*"

Spurred on by the order and the compliment, the little girl quickly grabbed two bottles from an ice bucket set in the shade behind her. She opened them expertly and laid them swiftly on the counter in front of Paul, who thanked her with a wink.

He paid Clara, took two plastic drinking straws, and went to sit with Mireya on a wooden bench under the shade of a tree near the canteen, facing the municipal building. He handed

Mireya her bottle, took a tortilla, and they both started to eat while sipping their drink.

They remained silent for some time, staying in their thoughts, and looking around as they enjoyed their snack. Mireya was the first to speak. Without looking at Paul, she said, "You shouldn't use that word *'compañero'* when you talk to people, especially in the presence of Ladinos... and even with Mayas, you know." Then looking at him and reading the consternation in his eyes, she added, "That could get you into trouble. And that includes those you talk to, like you just did with the workers on the scaffolding."

Paul couldn't believe it. "What? But I thought it was referring to camaraderie, fellowship."

"Yes, that's true. But here in Guatemala, the term is also associated with subversive activities, at least in the eyes of Guatemalan authorities. For them, the word *'compañero'* is also the equivalent of the 'comrade' associated with communists. Those who use it quickly become suspect."

Seeing that Paul was still staring at her in disbelief, she went on with her explanation. "The strike of seasonal workers on the plantations has made the government even more paranoid than it already was. You must be careful, there are always people willing to sell sensitive information. We call them *'orejas,'* the ears."

"Oh, come on, Mireya! Everyone can see that we're not doing anything wrong."

"If that's what you think, then you should know that some people in Guatemala consider missionaries to be more of a nuisance than anything else."

They interrupted their little debate when they saw a few young teens arriving on their bikes. Among them, Paul recognized Luis and Jorge from his youth group. They called out his name as they slowly passed by. Their faces lit up with a knowing smile when they saw that he was in the company of an attractive young woman. Jorge even winked at him. Paul watched them move away with a warm smile.

"The people of the village seem to have adopted you," Mireya said. "What are your impressions of the people and the country so far?"

"I haven't really had the opportunity to visit the region, and even less the other parts of the country. I only know Concepción and its immediate surroundings. All I can say is that I really like this place. And I love these kids... They are so natural. But I don't know the adults so well. I find it more difficult to approach them; I feel they want to keep a certain distance from me."

"I think this is mainly due to the fact that most teenagers and young adults speak Spanish, while older people are still reluctant to learn it."

"I am becoming quite friendly with José Alguilar, the schoolteacher. He has agreed to teach me the *Mam* dialect. Do you know him?"

"Oh yes, I know him well. We attended some classes together at the University of Quetzaltenango and became friends. José is a good person, and the people of Concepción hold him in high esteem. Did you know he was also a keeper of the Mayan Calendar?"

"I didn't know. I saw him assist the shaman Don Manuel in a traditional ceremony that was performed to seek forgiveness from Mother Earth before people began working their plot of land, but I didn't know he was also—what, a priest of the ancient magical calendar of the great Mayan civilization?

Are you saying that it's still in use?"

"Officially, it's prohibited, so people are very closemouthed when it comes to the calendar. But still today, most Mayas go to consult their shaman for marriages and baptisms and to perform special rituals, for example at funerals. In fact, I was told that José would be on his way to becoming a shaman himself."

"I am beginning to see that José is an even more important figure in this community than I thought. He speaks his Mayan language, Spanish and English; he's a shaman's apprentice, a keeper of the Mayan calendar, the village schoolteacher; and Father Callaghan told me he's also the secretary of the village council."

Surprisingly, as they were talking about José, they saw him coming out of the municipal building and heading towards them. He had obviously seen them from inside the building.

He joined them with a broad smile.

Mireya greeted him familiarly. "Well, speak of the wolf..."

"*Hola, amigos*! I saw you through my office window and decided it was a good time to take a break." Then looking at Mireya, "I heard that you are turning our social worker into a carpenter?"

"And me, that you would teach him your native language?" replied Mireya after glancing at Paul with laughing eyes.

"He is constantly fidgeting. We must keep him busy if we want him to stay with us."

Paul blushed, and they both laughed.

"Well, I'll leave you to it. I have to go back to the university," Mireya said, getting up. Then to José, "Oh, please tell me, how are Anna and the baby?"

"So far, so good," José answered while putting a hand on

his stomach in an instinctive gesture.

"Good! Tell Anna I'm thinking of her. Okay, Bye!"

Both men who had stood up to say goodbye, watched her walk away for a little while. Then Paul, wanting to avenge a little of their mockery, turned to José, pointing to his belly, teasing, "A little nauseous?"

José grinned knowingly and said, "It's mostly my mother who gets on my nerves. She won't let me stay at home. She always tells me to go somewhere else, where I can be useful instead of a nuisance."

"Poor you, let me know if there's anything I can do to help."

José didn't even hesitate and jumped at the offer.

"Well, that's exactly what I wanted to talk to you about in coming to see you. I thought we could visit some Mayan ruins not too far from here. It's not Tikal or Palenque, but it's not yet known to tourists, and it hasn't been restored. In my view, that's what makes this place so interesting. For you, it will be like discovering new ruins. I thought that if I'm going to teach you our language, I might as well take the opportunity to introduce you to our culture. Besides, it would do some people good, including me, to be away from home for a while."

"I'd love to. How long would we be gone?"

"If we can leave in a few hours, we could be back tomorrow afternoon, after a night spent on top of a Mayan pyramid under the stars."

"I need to check with Father John first to see if he might need me at that time."

"*Bueno*! If you can make it, be at my house at half past four. Just bring your backpack with a blanket and sweater for the evening. I'll take care of the food and refreshments for both of us. Don't worry if you can't make it, I'm going anyway. So don't be late."

The two then left the square, José returning to the municipal building and Paul to the medical clinic. After they left, Clara closed the canteen and soon there was no one left in the square. It was siesta time; even the leaves on the trees stood still under the blazing sun, as if time had stopped.

The Pyramid

The *colectivo* (a collective means of transportation, van, or minibus, inexpensive, of the underground economy) they traveled in, left them on a dirt road in a kind of no man's land, with no visible habitation as far as the eye could see. On the east side of the road, a path through a field of dried corn, standing like mummified specters, seemed to lead directly into a large grove of trees about a mile from the road, beyond which a small hill could be seen.

While José was busy checking their backpacks, Paul watched the *colectivo* disappear into the distance. Suddenly, the environment was plunged into a heavy silence, broken only by the noise of the fabrics rubbed by José and their own breathing. Paul thought that a silence typical of ancient times was being revealed again in this place. He felt that the air around him had become hotter than his own breath.

He stopped breathing for a second or two, looked around, and said, "Are you sure the place is safe?"

"I've been coming here since childhood. Believe me, you have nothing to fear."

He handed Paul his backpack and helped him to put it on. "I added a bottle of water to your stuff."

Then put on his own and turned toward the path. "Okay, let's go!"

Emerging from the grove, Paul saw that the trail continued through a more open area, dotted with flowering shrubs and bushes, before climbing steadily for a few hundred feet and disappearing into the forest ahead of them, then reappearing on their left along the hillside seen earlier, until it reached a white structure topping its summit. As they walked along the bushy trail, José explained that to master the intricacies of their language, Paul first had to understand their culture. He then began to teach him some of the names of things they could see around them, giving an idea of their symbolic meaning when appropriate.

But little by little, Paul had fallen behind. Ahead of him, the trail was getting higher and higher. José stopped at a point where the path split in two. On the left, it went up before disappearing again in the bushes, while dropping off rapidly on the right. He waited for Paul, who had adopted the pace of a long-distance runner, breathing at regular intervals, and keeping eyes to the ground. He smiled indulgently at Paul's contrite expression when the latter almost bumped into him. To reassure him, he pointed to the top of the hill.

"Look! We're almost there."

Seeing the steep slope that the path was taking to the summit, Paul's face grew longer; he motioned to José to wait a little. José took the opportunity to provide some cultural information. He pointed to the trail that went deeper into the forest on their right.

"You see that trail going down? That's an ancient stone path leading to a cave dug by humans long ago. Even today, people go there on pilgrimage. They come to pray and make offerings. They believe they can communicate with the spirit of the ancestors and get their help."

Paul looked successively at the path going down to the cave and the one going up to the pyramid.

"Why not start by visiting the cave?"

"It's a sacred place," José said. "Maybe another time, when you know our traditions better."

Paul looked José in the eye and saw that he was serious. There is a difference between folklore and cultural reality.

"I understand." Then he looked up at the pyramid again and said, wincing, "Well, okay."

José nodded, and they began an ascent of about three hundred and fifty feet, the slope getting steeper as they approached the summit. About halfway up, they stopped to recharge their batteries. Paul took off his straw hat and took out a handkerchief from a trouser pocket. He wiped his wet hair and the sweat running down his forehead. For a few seconds, he looked at José who had already resumed the climb. From where he was standing, Paul could not make out the shape of the pyramid. He only saw a jumbled heap of stones on top of a big mound of dirt covered with scrub. Looking behind him, he had to raise a hand to shield his eyes from the rays of the blushing sun that had begun to descend on the horizon, casting an orange hue over the forest.

He ended up joining José on the first of the two upper terraces that had been cleared on three sides. Only the back was still covered with earth in which vegetation had taken root. José invited him to come to the east side of the pyramid, where it towered above a natural pool of water framed by rocky cliffs on its other sides. Pointing to it, José started to give some explanations.

"This is a *cenote*, or *dz'onot* in our language. It's a kind of natural well, whose water comes from a lagoon located a little further through an underground connection. For people of the ancient times, this type of water source represented an opening to the inner world." Then looking at Paul, he added, "It's like a direct link to our collective unconscious, you see...

Paul nodded in understanding.

... We believe that the Earth is our spiritual mother and that all openings that allow us to enter within it are sacred—that applies to volcanic craters, *cenotes* like this one, lakes, and caves. And when we drink from this water, we say that we drink at the breast of our mother Earth."

Looking down again at the *cenote*, he went on, "You see the color of the water? It has a jadelike texture with a light green blue. This is probably why the jade became the most precious gemstone for our ancestors. The green of jade symbolizes the heart of the world, just as the water of this *cenote*...

... There's also the Ceiba tree, or Kapok tree, the national tree of Guatemala, which is represented by a jade-green cross. In Mayan mythology, the Ceiba is a sacred tree that digs its nine roots toward the Netherworld, the Mayan Hell, and strains its twelve branches toward the sky. We also call it *Yax Imixche* or *Yaxche*, the primeval tree, along which the dead make their way to the Heaven...

... From a more practical perspective, groundwater nourishes the tree, which in turn feeds the clouds, which feed the earth—and the earth feeds us. It's a cycle that the white man has broken by trying to conquer the Earth. There are ecological consequences of the destruction of the forests." Then looking again in Paul's eyes, "And this is not superstitious beliefs of gullible Natives; we are the descendants of a great civilization, and what our myths and legends tell is based on the lessons learned by our ancestors. Today, white people are just beginning to understand that the trees are the lungs of the Earth."

José suddenly became aware that he had been talking a lot.

"Sorry, Paul. I often get carried away when I talk about our beliefs and traditions. I hope I'm not testing your patience too much with my overheated rhetoric?"

"On the contrary, what you say resounds in me."

José then pointed to an eagle that had just appeared over the cliff overlooking the eastern side of the *cenote*. For a few seconds they watched it circle high in the sky above the forest before disappearing heading south toward the lagoon.

José's long monologue having allowed Paul to regain his strength, they were able to complete their ascent to the last terrace at the top of the pyramid where they found three stone altars. They sat on the central one and quietly contemplated the beautiful landscape that unfolded before them. In the distance, a layer of low clouds, drifting slowly over the Cuchumatanes, seemed to be set ablaze with sunset, the forest below gradually darkening. Soon they could no longer make out the bottom of the pyramid, but other lower mounds probably hiding other Mayan structures were beginning to loom.

José spoke again, keeping his voice down, saying, "I love coming here. And every time I do, all my worries and fears vanish. Here, I always experience a strong feeling of belonging to my people. In my youth, I came frequently with my grandfather and sometimes with my father."

"How long since your father died?"

"He died three years ago while working on a coffee plantation. The crops of our cultivation plot were not sufficient to feed our family; so, like many others in the villages, he had to work on the plantations to overcome the gap. There, they said he had an accident."

"Did you learn what happened to him?"

"He was working in the fields with a dozen others when a helicopter dumped pesticides right on top of them. They all died of suffocation. All native workers know that when the owners of large plantations decide to use insecticides or pesticides, most don't really care if there are workers there, especially if they are Natives...

... It was then that I decided to become a schoolteacher, stay in my home place, and try to help my people. Long before my father's death, I tried my luck in your country, like many others. I was fifteen years old when I began working there in the summer. With a group of older people, I was able to cross the U.S.-Mexico border illegally and got hired as a fruit picker in Texas."

"Didn't you have any problem with your age?"

"I was able to do the job and that's all the foremen wanted to know. After the harvest season, I would come back here and continue my schooling. Later, I was able to enter the University of Quetzaltenango, where I met Mireya."

José stopped talking, smiling at the reminder of that time spent away from home. Feeling disconnected, Paul took the opportunity to watch the last shimmer in the sky. Then he got up to look at the bottom of the pyramid, now shrouded in darkness. Curiosity tickling his tongue, he said, "I suppose that the pyramid served as an observation post like the watchtowers, but that it also had other functions."

"You're right. It's also a symbolic representation of the Mayan world. Like the Ceiba tree, the pyramid links the earth, the sky, and the underworld. Its square base represents the earth, and each side coincides with a cardinal point to which correspond a color, a tree, an animal, and a guardian spirit. Most of the time, it was the cunning of an animal which, having become an ally, provided the secret enabling man to live in harmony with nature. To conquer water, fire, nutritive or medicinal plants and to acquire techniques, man had to make a pact with things and animals. The pyramid was in a way the symbol of this necessary alliance."

Then José got up saying that it was time to get ready for the night because darkness was falling fast at this time of year. He asked Paul to go down on the other terrace to get some dried twigs and small branches he might find behind it. Meanwhile, José would light a campfire in front of the central altar.

They worked in silence. José's words had left Paul into a sort of stupor before the beauty and grandeur of this world. He was captivated by the living energy emanating from the surrounding nature. By the time he finished gathering wood and the campfire was well lit, the night had already fallen like a wall of silence over the Earth and the temperature had dropped. They put on their sweaters and wrapped themselves in their blankets. Finally, tired but satisfied after their long exploratory trek, they sat down leaning against the stone altar and quietly ate their meal of dried meat and a mixture of nuts and wild berries, while watching the stars twinkle in the celestial sphere. After a moment, José pointed to Venus.

"Our ancestors had synchronized their calendar with the heliacal rising of Venus, its appearance and disappearance symbolizing life, death, and the rebirth of the world. Their day-to-day life was keyed to its cycle. Each day was represented by a sign that the timekeeper could explain. Even today, some are still able to predict the future. But above all, the calendar has become the memory of our people. It reminds us that we are in a cycle of life, that we are living the end of a dark period of our history. It goes back more than 12,000 years in Mayan history and mentions several endings of the world and some great floods."

"But what does all this mean to you today as a shaman?"

"The shaman is also a Timekeeper. As such, I see myself as a guardian of the culture. I want to help my people stay connected to their roots, and to do that, I have to be able to read the signs of our time."

"Do people often come to you for guidance?"

"They mostly go to Manuel. But as I am his apprentice, some have started to consult me. They come to know the meaning of the sign corresponding to a date of birth, to choose a guardian ancestor's name that is almost never pronounced... It's like in the Catholic religion when you are given the name of a saint at baptism. But the minds of those who live in the capital or in the plantations become numb and eventually corrupted. Then they quickly become uprooted, forgetting their own traditions, and feeling completely lost. Most of the time they end up drowning their sorrows in alcohol."

Unwanted Intruders

A few days later, on a warm, sunny late afternoon, a lively music coming out from the health clinic could be heard as far away as the top of the hill facing the church. After a good day's work in the fields, people were heading home, chatting about anything and everything and swaying happily to the catchy tune.

Inside the clinic, Paul was busy painting the back wall of the waiting room. Perched on a stepladder, he focused on making a border under the ceiling above the entrance to the treatment room where Mireya was filling a shelf with medical supplies. A transistor radio on the floor played the song *'Ámame'* by the Argentinean singing duo Barbara y Dick. Mireya smiled as she heard Paul making a kind of swishing noise while trying to keep up with the music.

Paul was about to dip his brush into the paint pot on the pail shelf when he began feeling a slight but constant vibration under his feet. Worried, he dropped the brush into the pot and clung to the stepladder, which also began to shake. He grabbed the paint can, hurried down and went to turn off the radio. Bemused, on the alert, Mireya was staring at him. In addition to the shaking, they could now hear a kind of growing roar that seemed to be heading their way.

"What's going on?" Paul asked.

"I first thought it was an earthquake, but now it sounds like several heavy vehicles coming."

"Let's go out and see."

Stepping outside, they were awestruck to see a military convoy, led by two jeeps, and consisting of three armored fighting vehicles and a dozen armored personnel carriers, moving very slowly up the main street. When the first jeep reached the medical clinic, it stopped in front of them. Then, a soldier sitting in the back jumped out of the vehicle and, ignoring the presence of Paul and Mireya right behind him, began to signal to the other vehicles to turn right to go around the public square and join the village exit street, passing in front of the church.

Many residents had come out and watched with fear and suspicion as these unwelcome intruders passed through their township. Some of them rushed to the church. Paul and Mireya decided to follow them.

Father Callaghan was already on the church steps, watching the convoy that had begun to pass before him. Paul and Mireya hurried to his side. Paul's eyes widened when he realized that the soldiers crammed into the troop transports were in fact young Natives, whose faces had been blackened, presumably so they would not be recognized. It reminded him of what happened to Jorge's brother, who had been kidnapped to join the army.

The jeep that had stopped near the medical clinic now closed the convoy. As it passed the church, an officer in the back seat stood up, holding onto the back of the front seat to keep his balance. He turned to the priest and the others at his side, flashing a smirk, and then gave the military salute while staring at Father Callaghan with hate-filled eyes. They all silently kept watching until the convoy went away on a side road leading to the west coast, wondering what this show of force could possibly mean. The priest was the first to break the extremely tense atmosphere they were in.

He sighed with relief and said, "For a moment, I thought they were coming for us."

"They took a secondary road leading to the coast—probably to act against the striking workers on the plantations," Mireya commented.

"And they take that opportunity to intimidate the native population by passing through the villages they encounter," the priest added.

Then glancing at Mireya with inquiring eyes, "Did you know that almost no one from our parish went to the coast for this year's crop? That may sound odd, but it looks like they have smelled danger. It's mainly Ladino peasants and Natives living on the west coast that went there and are now on strike, those who lack the land or were dispossessed of their ancestral land. The picking is often their only resource."

"You may be right", Mireya agreed. "A rumor circulating among the university faculty and students says that guerrilla operations were carried out on some banana plantations."

"I would be surprised if the rebels had ventured that far," Paul said. "In the preparedness workshop I attended before coming here, we were told that only a few small isolated insurgent groups were hiding in the depths of the Petén jungle in the northeastern part of Guatemala."

Before reacting to Paul's comments, Mireya gave the priest a puzzled look, as if he were guilty of not having better informed Paul of the situation on the ground.

"I think the guerrilla forces are more important, better

organized, and more mobile than what you have been told. But in this case, I really believe that these are rumors propagated by government agents and intended to justify military action against the strikers."

"Did you see the way that officer looked at you?" Paul asked the priest.

"His eyes were flashing with hatred and scorn. He clearly identified you as an enemy," Mireya said.

Father Callaghan frowned but said nothing. He merely kept his gaze turned away to where the convoy had disappeared into the late afternoon sun.

Panzos

Later that evening, Father Callaghan took advantage of their daily after-dinner walk to share his concerns. When they reached the top of the hill in front of the church, the priest asked Paul if would like to pause for a moment.

The latter, still panting, but better able to keep up with the priest, did not respond, but hurried to sit on a flat rock next to Father Callaghan. The priest took a gourd out of his small backpack and handed it to his hiking companion, who unscrewed the cap, took a big gulp of water, then wiped his mouth with the back of the hand holding the gourd before giving it back to the priest who took a few small sips, screwed the stopper back on, and then kept the gourd in his hands between his legs, performing all these actions while staring at nothing, lost in his thoughts. After a while, he took a last look at the hill behind him where the convoy had disappeared, then gradually turning back to his left, he looked down the Tuipoch hill, then over the village to the church below.

Keeping his eyes fixed on it, he finally said in a deep voice, "I'm concerned. When the military starts strutting around like we saw this afternoon, it doesn't bode well. I have seen that kind of show of force aimed at intimidating the people in South America and Africa. Most of the time that means that a coup d'état is being planned or that a crackdown is about to be launched."

Surprised by the priest's tone and words, Paul tried to lessen his concern by repeating what Mireya had said, that the possibility of guerrilla involvement was only a rumor, and that the military operation was only meant to intimidate the strikers and protect the plantation owners.

Skeptical, Father Callaghan chewed his lower lip and asked, "You probably haven't heard about the events that took place in the village of Panzos."

"Panzos? Never heard of it."

"It's a Mayan town located in the northern province of Alta Verapaz, in a coffee-producing area. A few months ago, the people of Panzos organized a demonstration against the expropriation of part of their land to be given to retired military officers. Troops were sent in under the pretext of restoring order. The military encircled the public square where the demonstrators had gathered, and there, without warning, they began firing on the crowd. The bodies of the 119 people who were killed, men, women, and children, were dumped in a mass grave. Government officials claimed the troops had returned fire when attacked by communist activists."

"But this is pure barbarism!" cried out Paul.

"In Guatemala, the military are left to do what they feel is appropriate. Even here in Concepción, a body has once been discovered in a ditch along a secondary road, not far from the village. It was before my time. I was told that the deceased person was a ladino student from the University of Quetzaltenango. But what happened in Panzos marks an escalation in repression and involves the army, whereas previously it was a few isolated incidents perpetrated by paramilitary groups. Given the current unrest in the coastal plantations, this could well happen again elsewhere. This is Guatemala, a country ruled by a military junta. And it's well known that military governments have a marked tendency to fall into the trap of paranoia."

Seeing that Paul had no intention of commenting, Callaghan went on.

"Mireya told me that during his university years, José often wrote articles in the campus newspaper denouncing Guatemalan socialist intellectuals who denied indigenous culture when it came to the class struggle. Many socialist leaders think that the Mayas are included in the peasantry. The most radical ones even believe that the native people would be freed from misery only if their culture was to disappear. And José has always vigorously objected to this type of thinking. But I suspect that he has kept in touch with these people; he must consider their experience in the field of social struggle."

Then, while frowning, he sheepishly added, "We too are advocating for economic, social, and cultural liberation of Third World peoples, but Liberation Theology is a relatively new concept, and we lack experience. That's why I think we should take advice from José...

... Yes, I fear there will be difficult times. Threats, intimidation, and violence against them affect the Mayas less than before. They have become accustomed to a certain level of atrocities, one might say. They will not remain silent and not react well once the news of what happened in Panzos spreads throughout the country."

"But shouldn't the foreign officials in place alert the international community to condemn such crimes, to at least demand that those responsible for these atrocities be held accountable and to ensure that such abuses do not happen again?" Paul argued.

"Well, I'm pretty sure that the Panzos killing was not reported abroad. We must not forget that Central America remains the private turf of the Americans. I'm telling you, Paul, if countries like the United States can benefit economically from such actions, they will turn a blind eye and a deaf ear."

"But why telling me all this?"

"I want you to be aware of the situation. I can see that you and José are becoming friends, and he's a discreet man who doesn't open easily. He often goes to Quetzaltenango, and I suspect he has maintained contact with leftist intellectuals to help them understand the issues concerning the so called 'Indian problem,' which, in his view, remains a cultural matter before being a class one... And I would like to be better informed. I'm not asking you to spy on him, I just think he knows things that he doesn't see the point of telling me. If he opens to you, I hope you'll keep me informed of what's going on, if anything, to help us fulfill our mission and better protect ourselves...

...We, as missionaries, are facing a serious problem of conscience. In helping indigenous people to claim their rights, to protect what remains of their traditional lands and to demand being respected as human beings, we also bear some responsibility for massacres, like what happened in Panzos... We have to be careful Paul... as much for them as for us."

After these last words, they both remained silent, reflecting separately on what had happened and what had just been said. They remained like this for a while, gazing down at the darkening village.

A Letter from Paul

About 2,500 miles north of Guatemala, Louise, Paul's fiancée, walked out of her house located at the bottom of a long driveway leading to a country road near Camden, Maine. In the cold silence following the first snowfall of November, she was going to check her mailbox. To protect herself from the cold, she had put on Sorel snow boots, a wool tuque, and a hand-woven shawl which she held with her arms crossed over her chest. A light snow was falling and crunching under her feet as she walked up the driveway lined on both sides with tall pines and larches. She opened the metal door of the mailbox, slipped one hand inside, and picked up the few envelopes that she began to slide rapidly under one another. She stopped at the third one, breathless, as she recognized Paul's handwriting. She hurried home, took off her boots and tuque mechanically, without taking her eyes off the letter, left the other envelopes on the kitchen table, and sat down in a rocking chair by the burning fireplace. She took a deep breath, opened Paul's letter, and began reading:

Dear Louise,

Forgive me for leaving you so long without news. But please know that you are constantly in my thoughts. I feel as if I have been in Concepción for only a few weeks, although I have been here for six months already.

Everything went so fast. As soon as I arrived at the airport, Father John Callaghan, the priest of the parish where I was sent and who is my immediate supervisor, got me in his grip. In addition to my work as a youth animator in the parish and helping to set up a medical clinic, I must accompany Father John on daily early evening walks in the rounded hills around the village, where we are supposed to review the work done and discuss issues of concern. But in fact, most of the time, he takes the opportunity to tell me about his experiences during his years of missionary work in Africa or South America. So, my main contribution during these excursions is to listen while I'm trying to keep pace with him on sloping paths. The first weeks we often had to stop so I could catch my breath, and by the end of the day I was so tired that I often fell asleep with my clothes on. I've probably lost about twenty pounds since my arrival.

For a moment, Louise stopped her reading and looked up at the flame interplay in the fireplace, her mind drifting away, and she smiled as she imagined Paul, his pride hurt, struggling to keep pace with an older man. Then she resumed her reading.

Don't get me wrong, I'm not complaining; this is probably the best thing that could have happened to me. Before coming here, I was sunk into deep reflection, and I could not feel anything anymore. Now I can at least feel the pain in my body, and when I go to bed at night, I can't think of anything because I'm too tired.

Maybe I had to adapt to the culture and a different way of life before I could write this letter. I can hardly imagine the landscape around Camden which must be covered with a beautiful white carpet at this time of the year. The village where I work is about 3,000 feet above sea level, and the area is full of mountains whose peaks often disappear in the clouds, sometimes in trails of volcanic smoke. The houses are more or less of the Spanish colonial style with adobe brick walls and tiled or corrugated tin roofs. All the inhabitants of the region are descendants of the ancient Mayas, and the women still wear the traditional costume.

Even though they account for more than 60 percent of Guatemala's population, most indigenous people live in difficult conditions with few resources. They are often treated as subhuman by members of the dominant culture, which is composed of descendants of the Spanish conquerors and people of mixed origin called Ladinos.

I am intrigued by the Mayas. I feel there's a great underlying natural and spiritual strength in them that seems to protect their integrity and authenticity. It's difficult to describe. It's as if there's a special link that entrenches them in their native land. Beyond excuses to a god, the Mayas are aware of the wounds they will cause to the beauty of nature by transforming a forest with its trees, lianas and its natural indigenous plants that almost have a name and a function or a purpose. They are therefore doing so with humility and respect. They are constantly searching for harmony in all things; you could say they are looking for a complete balance between life and nature. And, of course, those they see as a threat to this desire for harmonization are seen as enemies. Just think of all that has been engulfed by the damming of rivers. Today I can better understand the distrust of Native Americans in North America or even the despair of those who feel or have been uprooted.

Here, I feel reborn; I've come out of my shell, and I'm opening to the world. I love these people, and I think they trust me now. I also think that I will never be the same again. A large part of the person I was that you knew died along with my brother.

You understand me, don't you? I could no longer make compromises to get back to a so-called normal life. So, I have chosen to follow the path that my heart has recognized. I don't know what will happen to me because what lies before me is unknown. I just hope I'll be able to bring something positive to these wonderful people.

I respect you too much to ask you to wait for me, so I release you of your commitment to me. Please forgive me if I make you sad.
With all my love,
Paul.

Louise was in tears when she finished reading the letter. She continued to look at it without seeing the words. She just muttered in a desperate tone, "Oh, Paul!"

A Soccer Game

A few weeks later, as routine appeared to have taken over again in the region, people no longer talked about the passage of the military convoy or the ongoing strike in the banana plantations, no one wanting to raise the subject. But this apparent calm did not prevent Paul from worrying about his youngsters.

He wanted to take their minds off things, to distract them. It was with this in mind that Paul and Father Callaghan decided to invite the community youth to have a friendly game of soccer on a clear day. José agreed to grant leave to his students and referee the game since Father Callaghan had insisted on playing as a goalie. The latter also suggested that Paul do the same, to offer fair and equal chances for both sides, as he put it.

So, on that sunny afternoon, they were twenty youngsters plus the two goalies and one referee, gathered on the dirt road running along the western side of the village, not far from the cemetery. Jute bags filled with sand were used as soccer posts.

The fun began before the game started, when Paul protested that Father Callaghan had put on his priestly cassock to guard the goals.

"Father John, what's the idea of wearing a cassock?"

"To show on which side God will stand," replied the priest, mockingly.

"It looks more like a sacrilegious act to me," countered Paul.

"That's certainly not for you to judge," added the priest to end the debate.

Everyone, except the priest, laughed heartily, then José called on the teams to play.

"That's enough now! Stop this childish talk and start the game!"

After the priest had stopped a few shots that should have passed between his legs, with his long cassock reaching down to his feet, Paul told José that he was considering filing a complaint of obvious cheating by the opposing goalie. The kids were having a great time.

At one point, Arnoldo, who was playing on Father Callaghan's team, bluffed the opposing defense and suddenly found himself alone in front of Paul. Surprised by his own feint and probably too nervous to make the most of this unique opportunity, he rushed his shot and missed the net guarded by Paul. The ball rolled about 50 feet until it disappeared into the ditch on the opposite side of the road from the village. Jorge, a defender on Paul's team, ran to get the ball, but stopped dead in his tracks when reaching the edge of the ditch, staring at the bottom, unable to speak. Alarmed by the boy's behavior, Paul rushed to join him. What he saw horrified him and left him speechless.

The ball had ended up on the belly of a mutilated body lying at the bottom of the ditch. Seeing their reactions, José turned to the other youngsters and told them to stay where they were; then he and Father Callaghan rapidly joined Paul to see the macabre scene for themselves. José gently took Jorge by the shoulders to draw him away from the scene. The boy burst into tears and buried his face in José's chest. After a few words of comfort, José asked him to go join the other kids.

From where they stood, the three men could see that the body was disfigured. The skin had been removed from the face, probably to make identification more difficult. They were all in shock. Paul finally turned away from the scene and vomited. José went down to take a closer look. Father Callaghan made the Sign of the Cross and followed him. They both looked at each other, and their eyes spoke of a tacit understanding; they had identified who it was.

"He was tortured; some fingers are missing," José said.

Father Callaghan began to pray for the repose of the deceased. José came out of the ditch and approached Paul.

Realizing that the latter had been sick, he asked, "Are you okay?"

Paul turned to him, looking dazed and confused, without saying a word. José reacted immediately by grabbing him by the elbow and adopting a stern tone.

"Come on, Paul! Pull yourself together! You have to take the kids back to the village."

"But we can't leave the body like this," Paul mumbled.

"I know. But for now, we must leave it there," José replied, glancing at the wooded area at the top of the hill on his right. "Someone may be spying on us right now. I'll cover the body with leaves and brushwood."

The priest, who had just come up from the ditch and heard the last part, agreed.

"José's right. Nothing can be done now."

"I'll come back with others during the night, and we'll take care of the body," José added. Paul finally accepted and went to join the teenagers, who now knew what Jorge had discovered and were silently waiting.

José and Father Callaghan watched as the group moved off, then they went back down into the ditch.

"Did you recognize him?" the priest asked.

"It's Eduardo. I saw him just before he left to make the rounds of his buyers. These are the clothes he was wearing."

"That's what I thought."

"His wife must not see him like this."

"I said the usual prayers. I know you will do the best under the circumstances."

He took one last look at the mutilated body, and left José, who began covering it with brush.

At midnight, Eduardo's mutilated body was still lying at the bottom of the ditch. Soon, slight noises of rubbing and of muffled voices approaching broke the silence of the night. Veiled by a band of tenuous clouds drifting slowly eastward, the moon dimly lit the scene, giving a waxy white complexion to the faces of the four men who had just emerged from the bushes and thickets lining the ditch at the foot of the hill. Guided by the hard light of a mini flashlight held by José, who remained at the edge of the ditch, the other three went down to retrieve the body. They wrapped it in a dark blanket, then lifted it up out of the ditch. José turned off his flashlight and helped the others carry the body.

Under the cover of the trees at the top of the hill, another man stood watch. He was looking in the direction of the group bringing the body toward him when a cracking sound put him on alert. He looked behind him at the winding path they had taken to make a detour in case the place was being watched. Hearing the muffled voices of José's group approaching, he sounded the alarm by imitating the owl's call. As soon as they heard it, the four men threw themselves down on the ground.

"What's going on?" a man in José's group asked in a low voice.

"I don't know. Keep it quiet! Wait for Octavio's signal," José snapped.

Octavio remained on the lookout for any unusual sounds. Nothing coming from behind, nothing on his right, but on his left, he felt that something had changed since the last time he had reached out in that direction. He focused his attention on a clearing at the bottom of the opposite hillside and saw the silhouettes of a group of a dozen armed people. The group crossed the clearing and quickly disappeared under the cover of the trees on the far slope. Octavio waited another minute in case anything else happened before signaling that the way was clear again with two owl calls. José and his group straightened up and joined him with the body.

"What happened?" José asked.

"A group of about a dozen armed individuals crossed a clearing at the bottom of the hill and quickly disappeared under the cover of the trees on the next hill heading north. Not soldiers... Maybe an ESA squadron or guerrillas."

"Fine, we're going in the opposite direction. We'll stay under cover until we reach the other end of the village. We'll cross over there. Let's hurry now."

José let Octavio go ahead for a few seconds to make sure that the path they were about to take was safe. Then he helped the others lift Eduardo's body and they set out following Octavio's steps.

Eduardo's Replacement

The next evening, Paul and Father Callaghan gathered in the priest's small living room. The latter had invited Paul to stay after supper on the pretext that they needed to discuss the situation. Looking at the seated priest, with his back arched and a lost stare, Paul thought that he had suddenly aged.

Graciela brought them coffee mugs and was about to go back to the kitchen when Father Callaghan said to her, "Thank you, Graciela. That will be all for today. You may go home."

She looked at him disapprovingly, her lips pursed, before abruptly removing her apron. She took the time to fold it up in front of them, put it on the table in the dining area, and left without saying a word.

As soon as the door was closed, Father Callaghan got up and went to fetch a bottle of brandy.

"A little brandy will help us get back on our feet," Callaghan said as he returned with the bottle and two glasses, while soliciting Paul's approval with a questioning glance.

He served Paul with a glass half full, took a sip of his own, and broached the subject that preoccupied him. "Did you know Eduardo?"

"Not really, no. I know he lived here and had a leather store near the town square. One day he even tried to sell me a horse saddle. He gave me the impression of having an easy-going character, of being someone who got along well with people, but that's all."

"Well said! But he was also an important figure in our community. He was highly active in the regional craft cooperative. At least once a month, he would bring an assortment of the cooperative's products to public markets that were widely frequented by tourists in Quetzaltenango, Chichicastenango, Santa Cruz del Quiche, the capital, and Panajachel, a resort on the southern shore of Lake Atitlan. He had earned the respect of the ladino merchants of Guatemala City and Panajachel, who bought his products to sell to tourists. He was doing good business for our community. People here have an expression to explain his business acumen; they say in their language that Eduardo had a 'protruding muzzle,' like a sixth sense in trading."

He paused for a moment, took another sip of brandy and then added, "I think we have just witnessed the beginnings of a new wave of violence and terror. And if community leaders like Eduardo are the first to be targeted, it's certainly with the purpose of cutting the ties that bind them together and destroy the bridge that they represent between the different communities. The aim is to intimidate people, to paralyze and silence them...

... The strike on the coast may mean that a broad-based solidarity movement is emerging. And such a nationwide association is what the government fears most... I called Bishop Urizar to tell him what had happened. He immediately cut me off and asked me to come and meet him at the bishopric of Quetzaltenango as soon as possible. He did not want to talk on the phone. I'm going there tomorrow."

Then the priest looked Paul directly in the eyes. He hesitated for a moment, seeming to weigh the pros and cons of what he was about to ask him. Finally, considering that there was very little risk, since it could very well be part of Paul's mandate as a cooperant, he decided to explain what he had in mind, and see how it would turn out.

"Now that Eduardo's gone, we need to find a replacement quickly, if only to maintain the economic health of the people in the area. But it won't be easy, and it could be dangerous, especially if the replacement is a Native. You know that they are often stopped by the police for verification. They must show their identity papers, are questioned, and even searched. And when they travel outside their district, they must have a pass signed by the military quartermaster or the district commander. So, I thought..."

Alerted by these last words and the hesitation of his interlocutor, Paul stiffened, and his eyes grew large. Anticipating what was to come, he interrupted the priest.

"Are you asking me to replace Eduardo?"

"Only until the situation calms down and the shock of Eduardo's murder wears off. Besides, as you are a 'gringo' there's little chance that you be interrogated by the police or the army. In any case, it fits well with your mandate as an aid worker, thus perfectly justifiable... So, what do you say?"

Reassured by Father Callaghan's explanation, Paul said he would be happy to help and that it would give him the opportunity to see the country.

Relieved, Father Callaghan smiled contentedly.

"Good! I expected nothing less from you... I will ask José to intercede on your behalf with the leaders of the cooperative. They are proud, but also very realistic. (Then raising his glass)

To the success of your new mission!"

Still a little stunned by his decision, Paul emptied his still half-full glass in one go and choked. He rose to his feet and struck his chest to temper the burning sensation radiating from his esophagus.

"A small glass of brandy can sometimes help keep your spirits up, but you shouldn't overdo it," Callaghan said mockingly.

Las Orejas

The following Sunday, the church being full, the doors had been left wide open. Many people stood in the aisles, on the front porch and outside on the forecourt. Father Callaghan had the impression that the entire population of the village and even the surrounding area had come to show their support to Eduardo's family. While saying Mass, he sensed that his parishioners needed to express themselves, to share their concerns and grievances. So, he decided to speed up the process of the celebration. After giving the final blessing to the faithful in attendance, he looked at Francesco, his beadle, and nodded. And while people hugged one another as was the custom at the end of the service, Francesco quickly went to set up a microphone on a stand in front of the balustrade. When this was done, the priest addressed the assembly through the altar microphone.

Having remained outside on the forecourt, right in front the porch, José and Paul were hugging those standing beside them, when they heard Callaghan's voice.

"My dear brothers, my dear sisters, we are all saddened by the tragedy that has struck us. So, I thought it would be good if those who wish to say something about what happened could come to the microphone, here in the House of the Lord, and share with Him and with us their pain, their fears, or their grudges. It's important not to let those things poison our hearts. If someone wants to speak, please come forward now."

A few people approached the microphone, mostly men. Eduardo's father was the first to speak. To encourage him, Father Callaghan said that everyone's hearts and prayers were with him and his family.

Eduardo's father cleared his throat and began to speak, his voice trembling with emotion.

"How long will we allow them to treat us worse than animals? They killed my son Eduardo because he was working to improve the lives of all of us. They killed him to scare us, to make us give up, so they could continue to kidnap our children and grandchildren with impunity and turn them into wild beasts. Last year they took my grandchild, who was not yet in his fifteenth year..."

In front of the portico, José and Paul were listening to the old man's words when José's gaze was caught by a man who had chosen this strange moment to leave the church. He knew the latter lived in the surroundings. It was the hint of concern he had read in the man's eyes when the latter had passed under his nose that intrigued him. The man hurried to leave the forecourt and walked away on the road leading to Tuipoch and San Juan, the administrative center of the county. José wondered why the man was leaving now. Then, he returned his attention towards the interior of the church where Eduardo's father continued to get it off his chest.

"... And now he is on a military base. You know they never tell us where they bring them, probably far from here. And there, they will break his spirit by cutting him off from his roots and force him to kill his own kind living in other parts of the country, where no one can recognize him. And later, he will not be able to return home because he will be too ashamed of having shed the blood of his brothers and sisters. He will gradually become a living dead, like you see more and more in Guatemala City. We need to react and find a way to save our children. The survival of our people is at stake."

Later that day, the man, who had sneaked out of the church, arrived in front of a small two-story building. Above the front door, a sign read *Oficina Militar de San Juan*. The soldier guarding the entrance stared intently at the fearful man appearing before him. Recognizing him, he motioned for him to enter. Once the man had disappeared inside, the soldier showed his contempt by spitting on the ground.

Two plain clothes police officers, one with his feet on the desk behind which he was sitting and the other standing with his back against the wall beside the desk, were laughing out loud when they heard knocking on the door. The seated officer shouted to enter. A guard opened the door to let the man from Concepción in. The latter stepped forward and stopped on the threshold, nervously fiddling with his straw hat.

Both officers recognized him immediately. The officer leaning against the wall straightened up, crossed his arms in open contempt, and waited with expectation for what was to come.

Leaving his feet on the desk, the sitting officer said:

"Well, well, well... Look who's coming to see us. Alfonso! Don't be afraid, come in! (Then to the guard) Close the door!"

Alfonso took a few steps forward and stopped again, still fiddling with his hat. The two officers exchanged glances and predatory smiles with one another.

"Come on, calm down; you could spoil your nice hat. Well,

I hope you have interesting stories to tell us."

Alfonso began to move his lips, but no words came out of his mouth, only an incomprehensible gurgle. Exasperated by Alfonso's dazed look, the standing officer decided to shake him by raising his voice.

"Come on, SPEAK! We have no time to lose!"

"Your Excellency, some er ... er ... bad things are ha-hap-happening in Con-Concepción," Alfonso finally manages to stammer.

Both officers suddenly became more attentive. The first one took his feet off the desk, straightened up in his chair and slowly put both hands flat on the desk. The other frowned and took off from the wall.

Reassured by the interest shown by the officers, Alfonso continued in a more assertive tone.

"At the end of today's mass, the gringo priest offered the people of the village to come to the microphone to express their resentment against the government."

"And what did they have to say against the government?" the second officer asked.

Alfonso moistened his lips and went on, "They say that Eduardo the saddler was killed because of his role as an economic development agent for the village and its surroundings. But they mainly complain about the abuse by the army. They say the army wants to destroy their culture by kidnapping their youngsters and turning them into wild beasts. They also say they will not allow this situation to continue without reacting."

"Anything else?"

"The blond missionary, the one working with the youngsters—Well, it is said that he is the one who will be replacing Eduardo."

"Um, hmm! Clever," muttered the second officer to himself, then turning to Alfonso again, "Is that all?"

"Yes, your excellency."

The seated officer then took a metal cassette from one of the drawers of his desk and placed it in front of him. He opened it and took a handful of silver coins which he handed to Alfonso.

"You did well, Alfonso. Keep it up and you'll be well rewarded."

"*Gracias, su excelencia.* You can count on me."

After Alfonso had left, the seated officer looked at his colleague and the latter said, "Maybe it's time to pay a visit to our friends in Concepción."

"Call Captain Sanchez!" ordered the seated officer.

La ESA

A ll the young people in Paul's group were sitting in a semicircle before him. He looked them in the eyes one by one. This was their first meeting since the discovery of Eduardo's body, and Paul thought that it was better to bring up this sensitive subject without further ado, to see how his youth had been affected and how they were coping.

"I think we should talk about what happened to Eduardo... It made me sick to see his mutilated body, to imagine the great suffering he might have endured. Before that, I never thought that someone could be so ... cruel. It scares me, makes me sad and mad at the same time. You see, it brought up different emotions in me."

Jorge was the first one to react.

"To them, we are not even humans. They regard us as inferior beings and treat us worse than animals."

"I wonder what kind of people can carry out such acts?"

"They are ESA killers," said Luis, Jose's brother.

"And what is the ESA?"

"ESA stands for *Ejercito Secreto Anticomunista*, the Secret Anti-Communist Army, a self-proclaimed right-wing extremist vigilante group," Jorge explained.

Paul, more and more amazed, slowly got up.

"But who told you that?"

"I heard José talking about it with Don Manuel," answered Luis.

Stunned to hear these young people talk so easily about these things, Paul sat down slowly and took time to digest what he had just been told.

"All right, then. Listen up! Everyone, including me, is pretty shaken up. And that's perfectly understandable and justified. I think the situation will return to normal as soon as the strike on the coast is over. But in the meantime, I think we should suspend our group activities."

The youngsters reacted by protesting vigorously, some on the verge of tears.

"If I propose to stop our meetings, it's for your own safety," added Paul.

"Even if my parents don't tell me, I can see the fear in their eyes. If we stop having our meetings, I won't be able to know what's going on and I might be even more afraid," Arnoldo argued.

"All right, all right, all right. But we won't do any more group outings until things calm down. You will be able to express yourselves during our meetings."

Everyone agreed on that.

Military Raid

A few days later, in the middle of a cloudless night, José and his wife were sleeping peacefully, their faces dimly lit by the moonlight coming in through the only window of their room, left open, when José woke up with a start, on alert. He thought he was awakened by an unusual noise. He focused his listening on the night sounds and soon heard a kind of humming getting louder and louder, like engines of vehicles slowly approaching. He listened for a few more seconds before gently waking up Anna and beckoning her to be silent and stay still. Then he got up and went to his window, which overlooked the main road leading to Concepción from the heights of the Tuipoch plateau. He partly closed eyes to better distinguish what he suspected he had perceived. What he saw then, gave him the creeps.

Dark silhouettes of a military convoy consisting of a jeep followed by four troop trucks were driving slowly, lights off, towards the village. The convoy continued to move forward until someone in the jeep, probably the commanding officer, raised his hand to signal a stop. The latter got out of his vehicle and was joined by the NCOs from the trucks. They talked for a few seconds and then each returned to his vehicle. The jeep and the first two trucks set off again in the direction of Concepción, and then several soldiers got out of the back of the other two trucks that had remained on site and regrouped behind their vehicles while awaiting orders from their respective leaders.

Realizing that they were going to be deployed on the trails leading to the homes of the people living on the plateau, José quickly returned to his wife and explained what was going on while getting dressed.

"A military raid. They know we are suspicious, so they decided to act at night. I'm going to get my mother. She will stay with you. She's quite capable of scaring off a whole army. Then I'll go down to the village to see how things are going."

Before he left, Anna grabbed his left wrist and urged him to be careful.

"Don't worry, they won't see me."

It was the same noise that had alerted José that woke Paul: the sound of an engine idling, but louder, closer. He sat up in his bed, turned his head to the window and listened carefully. He got up hurriedly and went to look outside, pushing back the curtain of his window slightly, just enough to see a military truck, headlights off, passing very slowly down the street behind the presbytery and heading towards the public square, then a second one. His heart tightened, thinking that this did not bode well for the people of Concepción.

He decided to go at once to warn Father John. The priest's room was on the courtyard side, so he probably had not heard the trucks coming. Paul put on pants and a sweater, did not bother to put on shoes, and hurried to the priest's apartment. He knocked on his door. No answer. He then tried to turn the doorknob. Seeing that it was unlocked, he opened it without further ado and rushed into Father John's room.

The latter awoke with a start.

"But what...?"

"Sorry to wake you so abruptly, but I just saw military trucks passing under my window. They were heading towards the public square."

"Oh, my goodness! An army round-up! They probably come to take our children and make them soldiers. Coming at night, they are sure to find them at home. We must hurry to ring the church bells. Maybe people will understand the danger and have time to hide their children. I hope it's not too late."

The mini convoy divided to cover the public place on three sides. The jeep and the first truck took a right to go around the square on the east side, the truck stopping in front of the building housing the agricultural cooperative and the jeep continuing until it stopped in front of the medical clinic. The second truck took a left along the north side of the church, then a right until it stopped in front of the municipal building on the west side of the square. Once all vehicles were in place, the commanding officer got out of the jeep. As he was about to give the signal to start the operation, the church bells began to ring. The officer held back his gesture and turned toward the church, with fire in his eyes. He waited for his lieutenants to join him before giving his orders.

"*Escuchad bien* [Listen up]! At the slightest sign of resistance, fire warning shots. If that is not enough, shoot those who refuse to comply. It will serve as a lesson for the others."

As soon as the lieutenants had left him to pass on orders to the soldiers waiting by the trucks, the commander stared back at the church, furious, and muttered through his teeth, "Damn Communists, I'll get you!"

Soldiers rushed into the streets all around, and soon after, they began banging on doors and barking orders. Then came the laments and the anguished cries of the inhabitants.

Jorge's parents lived in a small house on the street leading from the public square to the cemetery. They woke up to the sound of the bells. They were finishing getting dressed and Jorge was still sitting in bed rubbing his eyes, when there was a knock on their door.

Then they heard shouting, "*Policía militar*! Open or we'll break the door down."

While Jorge's father hurried to the back door, his mother grabbed a poncho and handed it to her son, urging him on.

"Quick, hurry up! Put this on over your pajamas."

After his father had checked that the way was clear outside, he turned to Jorge who had not finished dressing.

"Forget your shoes. Go hide in the cemetery."

Through the open door one could hear shouting and other pounding noises at varying distances. Jorge rushed outside just two or three seconds before the soldiers kicked down the front door.

Shortly afterwards, Jorge popped out of a narrow passage between two houses on the edge of the village and rushed across the small, exposed area separating him from the cemetery. He had just entered it when a shot fired from inside the cemetery stopped him dead in his tracks. By the time he realized it was a warning shot, he saw two soldiers emerge from behind a large tombstone. He looked left to assess his chances of reaching the brush on the other side of the road bypassing the village, but it was already too late. Before he could make up his mind, one of the soldiers pointed a gun at him.

"*Detente o disparo* [Stop or I'll shoot]," the soldier shouted.

Paul and Father Callaghan had just arrived at the public square when they heard the gunshot. Paul felt his blood run cold and his pulse race.

"My God, they've gone mad," exclaimed Father Callaghan, clenching his fists to control his anger. Frowning, he fixed his gaze at the jeep parked outside the medical clinic and said, "Come with me!"

They quickly crossed the square. As they approached the commanding officer, Father Callaghan turned slightly to Paul and whispered, "Don't say anything. Let me do the talking."

The commander was sitting in the jeep, quietly eating peanuts, pretending he was on a routine mission. He grinned evilly, his white teeth gleaming in the night, as he saw the two missionaries approaching.

"Ah, Padre. How are you? *Qué noche más bonita! Verdad?* [What a beautiful night! isn't it?]"

"What's going on? Why the shooting?" asked Father Callaghan through his teeth, struggling to control his anger.

"Probably a deserter," replied the officer, feigning disappointment.

The retort succeeded in making Father Callaghan lose his temper.

"Are you out of your mind? They haven't enlisted yet, they've become deserters?"

"You should be very careful about your words," replied the officer, also losing his temper.

Suddenly, they heard someone calling out Paul's name. They all turned their attention to the west side of the public place, where the voice had come from. They saw Jorge, escorted by two soldiers, followed by the boy's parents. The soldiers stopped when they saw Paul and Father Callaghan with their commander. Jorge and his parents looked desperate but seeing the priest with the officer seemed to rekindled Jorge's hope. He struggled furiously trying to escape the soldiers' grip, but they held firm. He uttered another cry of distress.

"Please help me!"

Feeling completely helpless, Paul could not meet Jorge's gaze. In despair, he cast an imploring glance at Father Callaghan.

The latter adopted a more conciliatory tone and said, "Captain, be reasonable. He is only 13 years old. You must intervene."

"Sorry, but you don't make the laws in this country. We all have to make sacrifices to give our armed forces the resources they need." He then turned to the soldiers who were holding Jorge and motioned to take him to a truck in which three other youngsters were waiting, staring blankly.

Father Callaghan placed his right hand on Paul's chest to keep him from rushing to the truck. Then he looked the commanding officer in the eyes and said, "May God have mercy upon you and forgive you."

The officer finally looked down. He'd had enough. He took a whistle out of his shirt pocket and blew three times. Then he turned to the truck parked in front of the cooperative, made large circular motions with his right arm, and yelled, "*Vamos!*"

The headlights of the vehicles whose engines had not stopped turning, lit up at once.

Father Callaghan put an arm around Paul's shoulder.

"There's nothing we can do about it now. Tomorrow, I'll talk to the mayor. I'm hopeful that together we can find a solution, at least as far as the younger ones are concerned;

otherwise, we'll never see them here again."

While Father Callaghan went to the parents to comfort them, telling them that there was still hope for them to have their children back, Paul stood still watching the truck in which Jorge was being held with three other youths from the village, flanked by five or six soldiers sitting on benches on either side of the rear section. After the last vehicle had disappeared from his sight, Paul could still see Jorge staring at him, tears running down, without saying anything.

When José arrived at the public place, he felt the anger rise in him when seeing Paul's haunted look.

Negotiation

Early the next morning, Father Callaghan, accompanied by Paul and the mothers of the children abducted by the army, showed up in front of the municipal building. They were surprised to find two military policemen posted at the entrance. Paul also noticed that someone was watching them from a second-story window.

"We've come to see the mayor," Father Callaghan said.

One of the policemen waved him in. "You, you can enter. The others have to wait outside."

To prevent any sign of protest, the other policeman unclipped his pistol holster.

As Father Callaghan entered his office, the mayor, a chubby-faced Mayan native, stood up and approached to shake hands. A framed photograph of the president and a painting of the Quetzal bird, Guatemala's national emblem, were hanging on the wall behind the mayor's desk.

"Ah, Father John, what a pleasure!" said the mayor, flashing an obsequious smile.

"Thank you, Mr. Mayor. As you can imagine, this is not a courtesy visit... I have come to ask for your help."

"Of course. As always, I will do my utmost to help you.

Please sit down."

Once seated, the mayor crossed his fingers as if to pray, and said, "What's the problem?"

"As you are undoubtedly aware, last night six young boys from our parish were taken away by the army." After that introduction, Father Callaghan fell silent, expecting a reaction from the mayor. The latter remaining impassive, the priest went on, saying, "Most of them are underage, and their families are rightly concerned about what may happen to them. We would be very grateful if you could help us get them back."

The mayor nodded and looked concerned. He took a few seconds before answering.

"You must understand that there is not much I can do... I am a civilian and this is a military matter."

Then he pretended to think about it some more and slowly gave a knowing look, as if an idea took shape in his mind. "We must provide the army with a plausible excuse, so they would not lose face or feel wrong. Let's assume some of the boys lied about their age to enlist in the military. But it would certainly be hard for the army to agree to such a solution; that would entail undue administrative constraints. They'll want to see birth certificates, for example, that sort of thing... well you know. And of course, that could lead to considerable administrative costs."

"Families are willing to pay, and the church will help if it's not enough."

"Who is the youngest?"

"Guillermo de Santis. He's only 12 years old."

"Hmm...it's quite young indeed... Listen! I'm not promising anything, and I imagine the army will demand at least 3,000 quetzals per person, just to open the files."

"I don't think we can raise more than 1,000 quetzals and we thought that would be enough for all six."

"Come on, Padre John, let's be serious. What do you think they'll say? After all, those little brats lied about their age, right?" replied the mayor with a wink, playing devil's advocate. "You can't seriously expect the army to let them go for only 200 quetzals a head. You have to think about the costs involved in recruiting them too."

"Perhaps we could manage to find a thousand quetzals for each one by soliciting donations from all the parishioners," Father Callaghan proposed, playing in the negotiating game.

"Um, I don't know. Look, if you can bring me the money by the end of the week, I think I can convince the quartermaster to look at the files of these new recruits, at least the younger ones. I'll do everything I can to get them back to us."

Having said that, the mayor stood up, and adopting a paternalistic tone, he concluded the discussion by saying, "You did the right thing by coming to me."

"Thank you, Mr. Mayor. I'll bring you the money."

The mayor watched Father Callaghan leave the office, before sitting back down with a little self-satisfied smile on his face.

Looking concerned, Father Callaghan went to join the others who were still waiting outside. He did not answer their questions right away, but hurried to lead them away, out of earshot of the military police.

Once in the middle of the public square, he stopped and addressed the women, saying, "Don't worry, it should be fine. Go home now. In two or three weeks, there's a good chance your children will be back, maybe with less hair, but in one piece."

After the women had left, Father Callaghan turned to Paul and said, "We must consider the boys as hostages held by the authorities. We'll have to pay a ransom to get them released. Unfortunately, I think that only the youngest ones will be able to be freed."

"How many?" Paul asked anxiously.

"Probably Jorge and Guillermo."

Going Beyond the Limits

A Good Cover

A month later, the people of Concepción had returned to some semblance of normal life, and it was time for Paul to resume Eduardo's activities as a representative of the cooperative. But Mireya wanted him to do something more.

Early that morning, she was sitting at her desk in the clinic, watching José pacing nervously, weighing the pros and cons of her idea.

Eventually José stopped, looking uncomfortable.

"It's too risky."

"You like him, don't you?"

"Maybe so, but that has nothing to do with it. Eduardo was killed because he was a leader of the coop. I don't think the ESA knew about his other activity. And you want Paul to distribute information regarded as subversive by the military police? In his country, distributing leaflets about workers' demands may be a common and legal practice, but here it's a different story."

"Listen! By replacing Eduardo, Paul would have a particularly good cover, and we can count on a secure and strong network of contacts... Besides, he doesn't have to accept."

"On the contrary, I am convinced that he will accept if you ask him. He's not really aware of the dangers he might face. If he were, he would go back to his country."

"Eduardo was murdered because he was encouraging people from other villages to join in peasant organizations and cooperatives to increase their power in the market for handicrafts. I agree! Some cases of disappearance have been reported, especially in the western part of the country. All these people were working in cooperatives, but it is always indigenous people who are targeted. Jim Coulter, who works with us on the West Coast, is a humanitarian aid worker just like Paul and he has never gotten into trouble. And I don't see why Paul should."

Running out of arguments, José started pacing again.

"On the other hand, I think there may be a mole in the village who is tipping off the military police. If that's the case, you need to find out who it might be and stop him from talking. That's what you should be worried about," Mireya added, while keeping her eyes on José.

José froze and stared at her with stunned eyes, thinking she was reading his mind, then his gaze softened, and he nodded. He was about to speak when Mireya motioned for him to silence. Paul had just entered the waiting room. He joined them in the office. After the usual greetings, José apologized, looking embarrassed, and left immediately to Paul's amazement.

"What's wrong with him? It looks like he's trying to avoid me lately."

"It has nothing to do with you. It's the short time that has passed between the recent tragic events, Eduardo's death and the military raid, that is bothering him. And you, are you okay? You seem preoccupied?"

"I am concerned about the fate of our youngsters. We owe much to John, who finally found a way to recover some of the conscripts, all those under the age of fifteen, including Jorge.

But I wonder what other bad surprises await us."

"You know, Paul, most of these kids have had either a grandparent killed because he wouldn't give up his ancestral land, a parent who mysteriously disappeared, or a brother who was grabbed for a forced exile in the armed forces. They are confronted early on with their oppressed status. What happened here happens quite often, too often in this country. It is rather you, Paul, who are not prepared to face these episodes of repression because you never had to deal with that kind of thing."

"Just seeing what was done to Eduardo has troubled me a lot. Such cruelty was unimaginable to me. But even if they've experienced this type of repression before, we cannot let this happen again."

"Oh, don't get me wrong, the Mayas have risen up many times in the past, and if the perpetration of these types of crimes doesn't stop soon the people will rise up again."

Mireya paused, as if to give weight to her last words, and then changed subject.

"By the way, I heard that you will be taking over Eduardo's activities as a representative of the cooperative. Are you comfortable with that?"

"I wasn't expecting this at all. But, in the end, I think I'm going to like it. It's a job that shouldn't take up too much of my time, just a few days a month. And it will give me the opportunity to see the country, which I haven't had the chance to do yet."

Mireya nodded, and said, "True. Besides, I think it will help clear your mind of the tragic events you've been dealing with."

Then an idea suddenly seemed to pop into her mind, setting off a spark in her eyes.

"Look, I don't have class this afternoon. What do you say we do a little recon trip? We could go to Panajachel, which is one of the main craft markets. I'm from Solola on the opposite shore of Lake Atitlan and I know most of the merchants in the area with whom Eduardo did business. I could introduce you to some of them."

Paul took a few moments to think about the proposal and then accepted.

"Why not, we could go on the motorcycle John has provided me for my work?"

"That would be great. A few more phone calls and I'm ready."

"Okay. All right. I'll leave a note for John, so he doesn't worry when he returns from Quetzaltenango. I'll be back with the bike."

Mireya watched him leaving the clinic, then she took the phone and called someone named David.

Reconnaissance Trip

In the early afternoon, they were driving on a twisty deserted road in the Guatemalan highlands. Even though it was cooler because they were traveling on high ground, the sun was shining down on their heads, and they had to be careful not to get sunstroke. Mireya had put on Paul's helmet, which he never wore anyway. She was clinging firmly to his waist. Paul had only goggles for protection. In the distance, they could already see the peaks of the three volcanoes surrounding Lake Atitlan.

As they passed a road sign indicating they were approaching the city of Solola, Mireya tapped Paul on his right shoulder and shouted to take the secondary road on their right. Paul took it and they vanished in a cloud of dust as they sped up on a dirt road that rises slightly but continuously through an arid landscape.

They drove a few miles without seeing anyone. Huge clouds of dust lifted by farmers plowing their dry fields with rustic hoes were the first signs of people they saw, and poor native peasants dressed in rags were the first people they met. Paul noticed that, unlike the people of the Concepción region, these people had no zoomorphic patterns to distinguish them from other Mayan ethnic groups. The few houses that could be seen had wooden or mud walls and thatched roofs.

After a left turn, they had to slow down quickly to avoid hitting a speed bump, set up across the road, right in front of the entrance gate to a military base, opening onto a hundred-yard driveway leading to a giant sentry box made up of two huge boots topped with a huge German spiked helmet, all covered with camouflage netting speckled with brown and green.

Through an opening just below the helmet, two sentries posted behind a pivot-mounted machine gun were watching them intently. It was like something out of a comic book, with the serious and intimidating look of the guards adding to the grotesqueness of the scene. Surprisingly, they responded to Mireya's wave. The military base meant they were getting close to Solola.

Before their departure from Concepción, Mireya had given information about the towns of Sololá and Panajachel, two places they would visit around Lake Atitlan, an area that attracted many tourists every year, ideal for selling handicrafts.

Sololá suddenly appeared to them at the foot of a medium-high hill. Mireya had explained that this town of five thousand inhabitants, built in 1547 on a plateau sloping down to the edge of a sheer cliff forming, at more than 2,000 feet high, a natural balcony above Lake Atitlan, was the capital of the district of the same name and the seat of a bishopric. Over the years, Sololá had grown until it extended on the side of the hill of which they had just reached the top.

From there, they could see the golden sunlight reflecting off the roofs of the elegant old colonial houses clustered in a downtown area crisscrossed with cobblestone streets. But on the outskirts were the same type of cob and thatch houses of the poor people they had seen on the road.

They slowly made their way down the rather steep slope leading to the city center through a poor neighborhood. On the way, a few children dressed in rags began to run alongside the motorcycle, begging for centavos.

The view was impressive. Paul felt as if he were diving into a three-dimensional painting depicting a majestic landscape with a large white stucco church in the background perched on the rim of a huge crater filled with greenish water, shimmering like an immense jade stone, surrounded by volcanic peaks.

Arriving in front of the church, they turned left to take the road along the eastern shore of the lake. They stopped at a lookout located three thousand feet above Lake Atitlan, slightly set back from a steep road running down to the lake resort of Panajachel. They dismounted and walked to the protecting fence at the cliff edge to find themselves in front of a panorama worthy of the beginning of the world. The body of water was surrounded by majestic volcanoes of almost perfect conical shape and sheer cliffs. Clouds stretching overhead seemed to come straight from the mouth of a huge volcano on the opposite shore.

Paul was speechless in front of the majesty of the place and the gleam in Mireya's eyes said her pleasure to see him so delighted.

"The Mayas say that the world was created out of this huge crater that plunges to the center of the earth. Many come here on pilgrimage to revitalize themselves," Mireya explained.

"It's breathtaking. I understand very well why people want to come back regularly to this site. We can only feel humbled by such grandeur."

Mireya pointed to the tallest volcano facing them on the opposite shore.

"Just in front of us is Mount Atitlan, which culminates at 11,500 feet. It last erupted in 1853." She pointed to the next one to the left, "And there's Mount Toliman, rising to 10,200 feet. Both are active volcanoes."

Paul's gaze lingered for a moment on the cloud crowning the summit of Mount Toliman, then glided down the volcano before continuing along the southern shore of the lake to an old Spanish colonial-style hotel located close to a dock where a small cruise ship was moored.

When they entered Panajachel, the downtown streets were crowded with pedestrians—mostly Ladinos and descendants of European immigrants, a few Mayan women, some ageing hippies in Native Americans clothing—coming and going, crossing the main street on both sides, interfering with vehicular traffic, including a few luxury cars, a school bus, and even a tall, attractive blonde on horseback.

Paul wove his way through the colorful crowd and stopped in front of a small European café, located at an angle facing the Banco del Ejercito building. The houses grouped around the bank were all Spanish style, with whitewashed stone walls and black or brown tile roofs.

Before getting off his motorcycle, Paul watched a couple of hippies passing by. The guy and the girl were dressed in Native American style from head to toe: embroidered belts, leather and wool bags, jade, and obsidian necklaces. Paul stared at them until they disappeared into the crowd, then he joined Mireya who was waiting for him on the sidewalk.

"It feels strange to see hippies in a country ruled by a military junta, especially since I thought the species was on the way out."

"It costs them almost nothing to live here and the military and police behave as if they don't exist... They don't want trouble with American citizens. Okay! I'll wait for you on the terrace of the café while you go to the bank."

Paul took off his jacket, handed it to Mireya, and headed for the bank across the street. Mireya went to sit at a table from where she could keep an eye on the bike. She was watching Paul walk up the few steps to the bank when a Mayan woman carrying a wicker basket approached her. The latter put down her basket and began to unpack a canvas bag containing hand-woven wool hats with colorful patterns. One of them caught Mireya's eye.

Meanwhile, Paul had entered the bank and was now standing in line behind a dozen people in front of the only open teller window. Seeing the teller open a shoebox filled with two large bundles of quetzals, which he began to count, Paul realized that that it would be a long wait. Frustrated, he gave a reproachful look to the nearby counter above which a sign announced *Cambio-Change*. Then he began to look around.

The space inside the bank was rather small. To the left of the three counters set side by side at the back of the room, a closed office was guarded by a soldier who looked more like a teenager. The latter was holding an Israeli Uzi machine gun as if it were an outgrowth of his body. He was staring ahead, on the alert, with one finger on the trigger. In front of the adjacent wall, another teenage soldier, also equipped with an UZI, was looking in the same direction, towards the entrance to the bank.

Looking behind, Paul realized that the two soldiers were watching the slightest move or sign made by a longhaired hippy man sunk into a chair near the front door. His face was hidden under thick glasses, revealing a strong myopia, and a curly beard. He looked more like some sort of vagrant who would have crossed the American border a long time ago without realizing it. Now he was trying to tie old boots, which were severely weathered. He was moving very slowly, obviously under the influence of some drugs.

Suddenly, as if prompted by the same internal signal, the two soldiers advanced in perfect synch towards the poor beggar. They stopped very close to the man, pointing their weapons at him. They stood there without saying a word, watching him get tangled up in his laces.

After a while, as the boots were still unlaced and the old hippie still didn't seem to be aware of the guns pointed at him, Paul could barely hold back the ghost of a smile before turning away from the scene to see that the line in front of him hadn't moved. The teller finished recounting the bundles of banknotes and gave a receipt to the first customer who left. The next one in line stepped forward and placed two new shoe boxes on the counter.

Paul winced when he saw two more bundles of quetzals coming out of the first box. He eventually became resigned to the situation and got lost in his thoughts. So, he did not notice the arrival of a new cashier who was about to open the next counter reserved for currency exchange. Seeing that Paul was not moving, one of the soldiers quickly walked up to him and poked him in the kidney with the barrel of his gun. Paul was startled and a brief glimmer of panic passed through his eyes before turning to anger that was quickly suppressed. With his gun, the soldier signaled him to move to the next counter, where the cashier was waiting. Before reaching the *cambio* counter, Paul cast a last irritated glance at the soldier instead of thanking him.

When she saw Paul come out of the bank, Mireya wondered what could have happened to him, as he seemed so upset.

"What happened? They wouldn't change your traveler's checks?"

"There was a long waiting line and only one open counter. After a while, I got distracted and didn't realize when they opened the currency exchange counter. Since I was the only foreigner, I think it was for me. At that moment, a young boy barely out of puberty poked me in the back with his machine gun to let me know that I could go to the next counter. I almost exploded in anger. It was weird and insane."

"They are probably young Mayas who were forcibly conscripted at a very young age. I heard that during their military training, they are required to sleep with their rifles. They learn to express themselves with their guns. When I think that we have become almost accustomed to these ridiculous demonstrations of military power, it's a shame. But, you know, you had nothing to fear; they do get very good with their rifles."

"Thank you, that's very reassuring," Paul retorted, shaking his head in dismay.

To take his mind off it, Mireya took out of her bag the woolen hat decorated with pink and green geometric patterns that she had bought on the terrace and handed it to him.

"Here! It's to keep your head warm during the cold evenings in the Highlands."

Caught off guard, Paul's face went from anger to embarrassment. For a moment, he fiddled with the beret and remained tight-lipped. When he finally put it on his head, Mireya could not help but laugh. Looking around and seeing a few amused smiles, he immediately took it off and nervously stored it in his shoulder bag.

"Wait till it's dark if you don't want to attract attention. But I assure you, it suits you very well," added Mireya, mockingly.

Unsure of how to react, Paul ended up saying, "Well, uh, thanks for the gift. I like it very much... So, where to now?"

"It's two blocks down to the lake."

They got back on the motorcycle and rode off slowly.

When Paul and Mireya entered the small craft store she had mentioned, a man in his fifties with a chubby face and a large Mexican mustache was standing behind a counter, presumably busy entering data into an account book. He raised his head to look at the two people who had just entered. He frowned as he stared at Mireya, trying to remember who this familiar face belonged to.

Mireya smiled at him.

"*Buenos días, Señor* Pacheco!"

"By all the saints! Now, what a lovely surprise. My little Mireya! Gee, you have grown... and transformed into a beautiful young woman."

"And you, you haven't changed. I find you as you were ten years ago."

They kissed and the man replied, "You are too kind," while casting an inquisitive and somewhat suspicious eye on Paul.

"This is Paul. Paul, this is Mr. Pacheco, who is the owner of this garden of wonders."

Paul stepped forward and they shook hands. Then the shopkeeper turned to Mireya, with a gleam of curiosity in his eyes.

"So, tell me, what have you been up to? I heard you were

studying medicine."

"I am finishing my last year of study and started working in a medical clinic in the region of Concepción. That's where I met Paul, who came from the US to assist the parish priest."

"Really?" said Pacheco, frowning slightly.

"Paul is a humanitarian aid worker, a lay missionary. In fact, he is a social worker. He works with the youth and helps me with the clinic. (Then locking his gaze on Pacheco's) He's going to replace Eduardo, until we find someone else."

"Eduardo Sanchez from Concepción, the saddler? (Mireya nodded) What happened to him?"

"He died of a heart attack."

"Oh, that hurts me. I kind of liked him, actually. He was quite a funny guy, an odd character. But most of all, he always brought me top-quality products."

"You'll get the same quality," Paul assured him.

Pacheco then pulled out a notebook.

"That's fine then. Here, I'll take this opportunity to prepare a list of what I need. If you're not in a hurry?"

"No problem," said Mireya. "We're planning a boat trip on the lake. We'll take your order when we return."

In the Shadow of the Volcano

As the small cruise ship left its boarding dock, Paul and Mireya, standing apart at the stern, silently watched the small waves of wake breaking and dying on the beach of Panajachel.

The captain of the boat managed to bring them right in the middle of the lake so they could have a 360-degree view of the surrounding landscape with smoke rising above small Mayan villages on the western and northern shores, and a few fishermen in dugout canoes along the northern shore. As they began to move slowly westward toward Mount Atitlan, Mireya pointed to the top of the volcano, whose mouth seemed about to swallow the sun.

About two thousand feet from the shore, they began to slip into the shadow of the gigantic volcano. This had a destabilizing effect on Paul, who simultaneously sank into melancholy. It was as if an emotionally loaded bomb, which had been buried deep inside him for a long time, had suddenly been activated and exploded without warning.

It was so strong that he did not feel the tears streaming down his cheeks. Seeing Paul's troubled look, Mireya had the intuition that he was going through a shocking and revealing experience. She didn't dare speak, but she couldn't help but gently touch his face. Her gesture surprised Paul and brought him out of his overwhelmed state. The fear Mireya had seen in Paul's eyes faded as his gaze focused on hers. He wiped away his tears and decided to open up to her and share what had just happened to him.

"I think I was kind of hypnotized when the reflections on the water started to change on the line between light and shadow. Suddenly, the image of Eduardo's mutilated body appeared to me as if it had risen to the surface of the water. Then the face of my deceased brother, Francis, looking at me with benevolence, replaced it. A rush of sadness and hopelessness came over me. It was as if I could perceive their distress: the one Eduardo may have felt when he realized he was going to die and the one my brother experienced when the only fact of living became a cause of intense suffering, and then their resignation and loneliness at the approach of death. I was both deeply moved and scared at the same time; I also felt drawn to a kind of morbid fascination with death, but that was swiftly replaced by a feeling of fraternal love for all beings, as if an invisible power was keeping us connected beyond our individuality, something I had never experienced before, and it is here and now that it arose."

Realizing that he had spoken to her truthfully from the heart about his revelation made him blushed and looked away. But he had time to register the tenderness and empathy in Mireya's eyes. Paul looked up along the volcano, which seemed to rise forever and whose summit was now disappearing into the clouds, and then back down to its base, sinking into the water. Finally feeling relieved to have confided in Mireya, he began to say more.

"This is the first time I shed tears for my brother. (Then looking at her) "Francis was my twin brother. But he came first.

And even though we were twins, I always thought of him as my elder brother and believed that he would always be there for me. So, when he took his life, it was like a big part of me was gone forever. I became numb to the people around me and could no longer feel normal emotions such as love and joy, even towards my loved ones. My life, as I had imagined it, no longer made sense to me. That's why I came here: to find a new way, a new purpose for life. A friend told me that spending time immersed in another culture could change the way I see the world and myself. And it works. Here, I feel like I've been reincarnated with the memory of my past life. You, John, and José have become like soul mates to me, and the young people of Concepción like my younger brothers and sisters whom I love and want to protect. And I wish I could do more for them."

"I think I can understand what you've been through and how you feel. You've made it perfectly clear. And Paul, I'm sorry about your brother."

Mireya paused for a moment to emphasize the sincerity of her last words and the seriousness of what she was about to propose.

"I'd like you to meet a good friend of mine who could help you do more. But to do that, we'd have to go to Quetzaltenango. If you want, I can call him when we're done with Mr. Pacheco, and if he's available, we could meet him tonight, but we'd have to spend the night there, probably at his house."

"Okay, if this works, I'll call John and let him know I'll be back in the morning."

Childbirth

A bit later in the afternoon that same day, as the sun was slowly disappearing behind the hill facing the church of Concepción and the few clouds over Tuipoch were set ablaze, José's house was the only one from which no cooking smoke could be seen coming out of the chimney. The reddish light filtering through his kitchen window added a dramatic note to José's attitude as he sat prostrate on a bench looking like someone in a stressful situation. Keeping his hands clasped tightly in prayer, he kept looking worriedly at the gap between the curtains separating the kitchen from his bedroom. Although he could only see furtive shadows, he clearly heard his wife's heavy breathing and moaning. Suddenly the face of his mother Christina popped out through the curtains, and looking him straight in the eye, she said, "Go get Pieta, the midwife!"

José jumped to his feet. He tried to peek at the bedroom, but his mother closed the curtains in his face without waiting for an answer. He took his wool jacket and said in a voice loud enough to be heard by his wife, "It won't be long!"

Settled in their bed, José's wife was ready to give birth. Despite a lull in the contractions, her sweet, sweaty face showed signs of fatigue and she continued to breathe at a rapid pace. Standing by her daughter-in-law's bedside, José's mother dipped a cloth in a vase filled with water, quickly wrung it out and applied it to Anna's forehead.

"You're doing great. Pieta will be here soon. After that, things will go quickly."

"Where's José?"

"He went to fetch Pieta."

Suddenly they heard noise and muffled voices coming from the front of the house. Christina went to look.

"It's them coming."

As soon as she entered, Pieta, who was an imposing figure with her strong build and angular face, turned to José to prevent him from passing. The latter wanted to sneak in, but the furious look that Pieta gave him stopped him short.

"No, you don't. Now you must do what needs to be done."

It was not the time to confront the midwife. José lowered his head, visibly upset, but did not insist.

"Okay, okay! I'll be at Manuel's."

Upon hearing Pieta's voice, Anna and Christina exchanged a hopeful look. Pieta nodded at Christina and walked straight to Anna. She placed her hand on Anna's forehead and looked into her eyes. Then, still without saying a word, she put her hands on Anna's belly, and after looking under her gown, she announced: "Baby's coming."

José discreetly knocked on the door of a house a little apart from the others. The door opened almost immediately, revealing the face of the old shaman.

Reading the emotion on José's face, Manuel exclaimed, "Ah, the baby is coming!" José could only nod. Manuel patted him on the shoulder with a smile and pulled him inside.

"Come, come. Everything is ready. I was expecting you."

Inside the house, the two men worked over a kitchen table that had been transformed into a makeshift altar. They began by lighting candles in wooden holders that had been placed on a red tablecloth decorated with green zoomorphic motifs. A black wooden cross was on the wall behind the altar.

Manuel poured the contents of a hollowed-out calabash directly onto the altar table. The mixture spread out on the table included maize grains, coffee beans, and seeds. Manuel carefully examined the morphology of the whole, then announced, "It's a boy."

He remixed the whole thing and poured it back on the table. After having carefully analyzed the new structure, he added, "Maize also says that your child will have all his limbs and be sane. That's all I can say for the time being. Now, you must pray at the three sacred places: at this altar, at the cross in the church, and at the cave where we will go together to ask the ancestors for protection. The ceremony will be important for you as well, as it will officially consecrate you as a shaman and spiritual leader of our community. Now let's pray!"

Manuel and José knelt before the makeshift altar, facing the black cross, their heads slightly bent forward, bringing their chins close to their chests as a sign of humility, and both began to whisper a prayer in unison.

The baby came at about the same time. Tired, exhausted, Anna had closed her eyes, but her face lit up when she heard the newborn's crying and screaming.

Tecum Uman Day

It was happy hour time in Guatemala when Paul and Mireya arrived at the main square in downtown Quetzaltenango, and the place was quite busy before the evening meal. Leaving the motorcycle in a safe place, they took *11 Avenida* along the east side of the *Parque à Centro America*, passed the *Catedral del Santo Espiritó* and stopped for a few minutes to listen to a group of Ladino musicians play a Spanish serenade on bamboo xylophones.

When they crossed the street to the urban park, the musical soundscape suddenly turned into true cacophony as the sound of xylophones mingled with the wind instruments and steel drums of a military band performing in a bandstand in the center of the square.

The place happened to be a lovely park, partially wooded, perfect for a pleasant evening stroll, with its bandstand and a large fountain, but frequented almost exclusively by Ladinos from wealthy families and a few tourists. As there was already a lot of activity before the evening meal, Paul and Mireya quickly made their way to the fountain near which they could sit on a stone bench, not far from the musicians. From there, they could finally identify what piece of music the band was playing; it was a lame version of "New York, New York" that made Paul smile, while Mireya, with a disgusted look on her face, stated it was pathetic.

On the sidewalk along the west side of the park, a group of Mayas were looking at the scene, perplexed. Right behind them, a white man was staring intently at Paul and Mireya. When she finally felt the weight of this intense gaze, she turned in his direction, and the man gave her a barely perceptible nod.

By 8:00 p.m., darkness had begun to set in, and streetlights were on. Sitting on the terrace of a café-restaurant overlooking the main square, Paul and Mireya had just finished their evening meal. Their waiter, a young ladino in traditional Mayan dress, had cleared the table and was now coming back with a pot of coffee. He filled their cups, left the coffee pot on the table, and let them enjoy the view they had on the park. From where they were, they could still hear music coming from the bandstand, but the remoteness and hubbub of the growing crowd, which had begun to invade the public square and surrounding streets, made it almost impossible for them to recognize what was being played.

Paul took a sip of coffee and then glanced at the ever-growing crowd.

"It feels so strange to be here in Quetzaltenango. I had almost forgotten that this country has another face."

"Most Ladinos have little or no contact with the Maya, and when they do, they ignore them. They persist in believing that the Maya have remained in a state close to savagery, still uncultivated, barbaric, and having evolved little since the Conquest. But deep down inside, they still fear the legendary power of the ancient Maya civilization, and the government does everything in its power to keep them outside modernity. Few own a television or household appliances. And those who have tried to change things have been seriously repressed."

"And you think that's why Eduardo was killed?"

"To me it's a certainty. Eduardo was a nice guy, always laughing and in a good mood. His death is a terrible loss to his community and the cooperative. We must identify those who murdered him and those who gave the order, and then inform both the local population and the international community. We need external assistance to keep our country peaceful. But for that, we need the help of people like you, Paul.

"Who's 'we'?"

"I am a member of an organization called *Comité de Unidad Campesina*, or CUC, the Committee for Peasant Unity. It was people from the CUC who initiated the strike at the banana plantations. We are a newly formed, peaceful group, and currently conduct most of our activities underground. Among other things, we demand equitable land reform, social and economic justice for all, and broad representation of the different Mayan groups before the government. We also want to see an end to the abuses committed by the army and military militia against the civilian population. Our main weapon is a small newsletter that we publish under the title *Justicia y Paz*. And that's it!"

"I am impressed! You say I could help you; yes, but how?"

Mireya was about to answer when their conversation was suddenly interrupted by the wail of a police siren. She understood almost immediately what it meant and smiled at Paul to reassure him.

"I forgot that today, March 19, is Tecum Uman Day, which commemorates the decisive victory of Alvarado over the last great Mayan leader, Tecum Uman. The outcome of this battle put an end to the war of Spanish conquest over the Mayas. The siren announces the beginning of the festivities."

As the siren sounded again, a man, his upper body covered with a wooden and papier-mâché frame, representing a bull with its horns, emerged from an alley between two buildings. The bull man ran down the street in circles, bobbing his head. Fireworks attached to his horns took off, whistling and backfiring, while other fireworks swirled around, spitting sparks. He then rushed to the front of the terrace where Paul and Mireya sat. There, he began to move back and forth, stopping abruptly, each time throwing a shower of sparks, while several youngsters tried to stay as close as possible to the beast, screaming with excitement and jumping to avoid the flying sparks.

While Paul was mesmerized by the frenzy taking place before them, Mireya used a cavernous voice to comment on the scene, "Alvarado faced the demon in the form of a roaring bull, outwitted his evil tricks, and beat it."

The fake bull finally disappeared in a cloud of white smoke. The siren sounded again and a new bull coming out of the same alley began to provoke the reckless youngsters with vigorous headbutts. Mireya smiled as she watched the youngsters fearfully approach the new bull filled with sparkling fury.

"I know it's foolish, but I love it. With my brothers we used to come over here every year to participate in the Tecum Uman Day celebrations. I still see us facing the bull, trying not to jump while the sparks were coming towards us, until we ran away, screaming as if we had the devil at our heels."

While they were enjoying themselves as they watched the young people run away from the fireworks, the man who had waved to Mireya earlier in the park approached their table.

Before they realized his presence, he announced himself,

"*Buenas tardes,* Mireya."

Paul and Mireya turned to see the newcomer.

"Ah! David. I'm glad you could come. Paul, this is David Steiner."

Paul stood up and the two men shook hands.

"I am delighted to meet you, Paul. José has told me a lot about you. I've been looking forward to meeting you."

Disconcerted, noting the obvious connection between Mireya, José and this man, Paul looked at them suspiciously one after the other before addressing David.

"You know José?"

Surprised by Paul's reaction, David looked at Mireya with questioning eyes.

"We had just started talking about the organization when the festivities interrupted us," Mireya explained.

"I understand," David answered. (Then smiling at Paul) "Can I sit down?"

Still a little confused, wondering what was going on, Paul reacted automatically, without thinking. "Of course."

David pulled out a chair and sat down.

"I teach sociology at the University of Quetzaltenango. That's where I met José and Mireya. All three of us are members of a pacifist organization, and we thought you might be willing to help us."

"Mireya told me a bit about what you do. What kind of help do you expect from someone like me?"

"If you don't mind, I'd prefer we discuss this elsewhere. I suggest you finish your coffees, and we go for a walk."

An Unpleasant Incident

A little later, the three of them were quietly walking up a small, poorly lit cobblestone street. The muffled sound of the festivities could still be heard in the distance. There was no one else on the street, and David took the opportunity to tell his story.

"My grandfather fled occupied France during World War II and eventually settled in Guatemala. In the 1950s, he served as a political advisor in the socialist government of President Arbenz, the only truly democratic government this country has known. He was executed following the coup that brought down that government. Since then, the country has been governed by a succession of military dictatorships, most of which have been imposed by other coups. I followed in my father's footsteps in teaching."

Suddenly, a door opened violently in front of them on a drunken Ladino soldier being expelled from a smoky speakeasy, letting laughter and voices filter out over a background of light and lively music. The soldier stumbled and fell to his knees in front of Paul, clutching Paul's jacket. When he bent down to help him up, the soldier suddenly straightened up and pushed Paul away, who almost fell on his back.

"*Basta ya!*" Mireya cried out. You are drunk, soldier! What a disgrace!"

To hear the voice of a woman shouting at him, seemed to ring a bell in the head of the soldier. He regained his senses a little and began to look at Mireya from head to toe with wonder and excitement, lingering insolently on the curve of her breasts. He then went up to the eyes of the young woman, giving her a naughty smile.

Seeing Mireya's face wince in anger, David took her by the arm.

"Come on, let's get the hell out of here!"

"And you, you'd better go home," Paul told the soldier.

To which the soldier replied in an aggressive tone, "*Ay el rubio. Gringo rubio.* Yes! Run home to mummy."

Without turning around to answer the soldier, Paul caught up with David and Mireya, who had started to walk away, and they took a side street.

Realizing they had disappeared, the soldier cried out, "Hey Gringo, come back! I was joking. I'll buy you a drink."

When he realized that they were not coming back, the soldier went back to the bar door and started pounding on it with his fists.

The CUC

Later that evening, David, Paul, and Mireya were sitting around a small wooden round table in the kitchen of David's house, where David and Mireya silently waited for Paul to finish flipping through the last issue of their little ten-page newspaper. A headline announcing the massacre of a Mayan Chuj village along the Guatemala-Mexico border grabbed Paul's attention. The article included a photo showing the remnants of the village that had been burned down. He took the time to read the article before closing the publication, keeping his eyes fixed on the paper's name, *Justicia y Paz*, printed in large red letters.

"Why red for a title like Justice and Peace?"

"A lot of innocent blood has already been shed in Guatemala, and in light of past experiences, we believe that we are on the verge of seeing blood spilled again if nothing is done to prevent it," explained Mireya. "In fact, it has already started in a few remote places, including the incident in the Chuj village, as reported in our newspaper."

"How did you get the information about this village?"

"Most of the information comes from refugees who have managed to cross the Mexican border. Once again, it's the same scenario all over again. Community leaders begin to disappear mysteriously and sometime later the people rebel and the army intervenes to restore, allegedly, civil order. In that case, the army made sure to close the area to outsiders and then nipped the rebellion in the bud by wiping out a few villages by bombing them with napalm and the soldiers killed those who tried to flee. Very few succeeded to cross the border. You see, what happened to Eduardo is just the beginning of that process. We must act before the situation gets any worse."

David, taking over, "We want to spread information like this outside the country to discredit the Guatemalan government in the eyes of the international community and to call on other countries to exert pressure and prevent a new genocide."

Then Mireya went on, saying, "And of course, we also want to disseminate information to the different Mayan communities, with the aim of creating a network that would allow them to speak with one voice. If this were to happen, we believe the government would have no choice but to listen."

"So, what exactly do you want from me?" Paul asked again.

"Contact had been made in most of the communities surrounding your area. Since you will replace Eduardo as the representative for the regional cooperative, you will need to go to most of the villages in the Concepción area where Eduardo had already established contacts. This legitimate activity could be used as an excellent cover for other activities, such as distributing our publication and passing on useful information to local leaders who would then inform their people."

"There would be only one copy of the newspaper to be given to each local leader, who would burn it before communicating its contents verbally in small groups," David added.

"So, Paul, would that be okay with you?" Mireya asked.

"Not only do I accept, but I also appreciate the opportunity to join in and do my part."

David then got up and fetched a bottle of rum and three measuring glasses. He filled them to the brim and distributed them. He then raised his and called out in a loud voice, "*Justicia Y Paz!*"

Paul and Mireya did the same, and they all repeated "*Justicia y Paz*" in unison.

Seeing that the others had emptied their glasses in one go, Paul almost choked trying to imitate them. David and Mireya broke out laughing.

David refilled their glasses, saying to Paul, "The first shot clears the way, and the others go down smoothly."

A Tribute to the Ancestors

The next morning, two human silhouettes appeared in the dawn light on the path running through the same cornfield that Paul and José had taken to get to the pyramid. But this time it was José and the shaman Manuel going to the sacred cave under the pyramid to pay tribute to the ancestors and ask for their protection for the newborn.

The shaman was leading the way. When they reached the fork where the main path continued uphill on their left up to the pyramid, they went straight on the small path that went down on their right and disappeared into the forest. A little further on, the trail became more and more rocky as it skirted the uncleared mound of about fifteen feet in diameter hiding most of the pyramid. Over time, shrubs and brush had grown on the grassy knoll and between large, mossy boulders littering the edge of the trail. During the whole trip, they remained silent, Manuel always keeping his eyes fixed on the way ahead, concentrated on the task at hand, while José seemed more feverish, listening for unusual sounds, rather rare in this stifling atmosphere. He was looking nervously around him, left and right, up and down, disturbed by the ambient dampness and the strange calmness of the place.

The trail ended at the *cenote*, the natural well adjoining the base of the great structure. The entrance to the cave, partially hidden behind the brush, seemed to go down under the pyramid. Once there, they took a short break to quench their thirst and mop up the sweat from their faces and necks.

Before entering the cave, the entrance to which corresponded to the size of a man of average height, Manuel took out some effects from a canvas bag embroidered with animal motifs, including a small clay pot with a chain, bits of pine wood, a bottle containing copal resin, and another one with pine resin. He put the pieces of wood and some pebbles collected in front of the cave entrance into the pot and then coated them with the resins.

José was carefully observing all of Manuel's actions. When these preparations were completed, the shaman turned to José to explain what he was doing.

"You see, these small pebbles are the guardians of this opening that gives access to the world of Xibalba, where our ancestors returned. By setting these stones on fire, I will awaken them and ask them to intercede for us with the spirits of the Underworld."

José having nodded understandingly, Manuel lit the mixture he had prepared in the clay pot. Soon a thick black smoke rose, and the shaman started chanting a prayer while swinging his makeshift censer in front of the cave entrance.

"Oooo Xibalta, Oooo Tiox Mundo, Santo Mundo, forgive us for coming to disturb your sleep and I beg you, allow us to enter, me Manuel Ochte and my apprentice José De leon Ochte. Oooo Xibalta, Oooo Tiox Mundo, I beg you, grant us to meet the spirits of our ancestors to whom we ask for protection for José's newborn son."

While continuing to swing his censer and mutter, Manuel slowly entered the cave. José followed, and soon the two disappeared, hidden by the column of black smoke coming out of the cave.

Hangover

Later that morning, Father Callaghan was chatting with his beadle in the rectory courtyard when they heard Paul's motorcycle approaching. They fell silent and turned to the entrance of the courtyard to watch for his arrival. Although the priest was relieved to see him return, he squinted his eyes and pursed his lips to make himself look stern as he watched Paul get off the bike. When the latter took off his helmet and old goggles, the others could see how exhausted he was from his escapade. With his shaggy hair, eyes weighed down by dark circles, and a face blackened by the diesel fumes from the buses he had had to follow on the road, Paul looked ten years older.

The moment Paul turned off the motorcycle engine, Father Callaghan greeted him coldly, saying mockingly, "I hope your little escapade allowed you to recharge your batteries?"

Paul looked at him with a sad and guilty look. Before he could open his mouth to apologize and explain himself, Father Callaghan pointed to the beadle and added in a vengeful tone, "Francesco was about to go to the mountain to get some firewood. I would have liked to help him, but I woke up with a bad back because yesterday I fell asleep in my chair waiting for your phone call. I think that Francesco would appreciate very much if you could give him a hand."

Paul hesitated for a moment, but he didn't really have a choice.

"Uh... (Clearing his throat) Yes, of course. Look John, I'm sorry, I forgot to call. I'll get my hat and some water."

While Paul had begun the arduous climb up the rounded hill in front of the church and was already struggling to keep up with Francesco's pace, José and Manuel were standing at the bottom of the cave, bare-chested and face blackened, in front of the still smoldering remains of a ritual fire that Manuel had fed with pieces of resin-coated pinewood.

Manuel squatted down to examine the remains of his offering more closely. After a few seconds, he revealed in a deep voice what he had perceived.

"If the baby is still alive after the first twenty days after birth, and as he was born on a *Caban* 9, according to the ancient Mayan calendar, he will bear the Mayan name of Caban, and the number nine, which is dedicated to the Creator of all things, will be his magic number. He will experience dark days, face fire, but will be strong and become a natural leader. He will be a good guide for our people. He will help them out of their torpor and prepare them for the new times of the next Baktua, which will begin on the winter solstice of 2056, according to the Long Count Calendar. The end of our torments is near, and those who stole our land will be punished."

Having finished saying what he had seen through the remains, Manuel left his formal and serious role. He stood up, smiled broadly, looked at José, and asked, "Have you chosen the name he will officially bear?"

"We have decided to name him Arturo in memory of my father."

Moved by this choice, Manuel nodded and said, "It's a very

good choice and that makes me very happy!"

It was almost noon when Paul and the beadle, both loaded as mules, emerged from a wooded area on a hilltop. Paul walked painfully, his face sweaty, his upper body bent to the ground. He stopped, gazed up at the sun at its zenith, and then looked ahead, trying to assess how far they still had to go. They would have to walk down the hillside they were on, up another hill and then back down again before reaching their destination.

Sweating more and more under the blazing sun, his eyes becoming irritated by the flow of sweat, Paul, visibly suffering, looked at Francesco who had already started to descend. The beadle turned to see if Paul was following. The latter removed his straw hat, took out a handkerchief and wiped his forehead and eyes with it, before spreading it on his head. Then he put his hat back on, took a good sip of water from his gourd hanging over his chest, and motioned to the beadle to continue. He sighed and set off again, with his bed in mind as a motivator.

By mid-afternoon, Paul was lying on his bed, fully clothed, with a damp towel on his forehead, in the muted light of day filtering through the curtains of his window. Even if it was open, it didn't let any sound through, as if the whole village had been deserted; only the curtains were silently undulating under a gentle breeze. So, Paul clearly heard a discreet knock on his door.

He immediately opened his eyes and raised himself on an elbow.

"Yes?" he asked in a raspy voice.

The door opened just enough to reveal José's face.

"Ah, José, please come in!"

"Graciela told me you were in your room," José excused himself on entering. He closed the door and then noticing the

141

wet towel on Paul's forehead, he asked, "Are you sick?"

Paul pointed to the chair at his desk. "Please sit down."

As José pulled out the desk chair and sat down, Paul leaned up against the wall at the head of his bed, and then he told his story.

"Yesterday, Mireya took me on a tour of some of the craft cooperative's clients. After visiting Panajachel, we went to Quetzaltenango where we met David Steiner. We stayed overnight at his place, talking almost all night long about the CUC and their newspaper—while drinking rum. I completely forgot to call John, as was planned, to tell him I wouldn't be back until today. He greeted me rather coldly when I arrived this morning and sent me into the mountains to fetch wood with Francesco. It was tough. I'm exhausted. I think I drank too much, have not had enough sleep, and I probably got sunstroke."

"Oh! He didn't go easy... Late last night, he asked for me. He was very worried," José explained. "He was quite concerned about you. I told him not to be worried, that you went on tour with Mireya, and knowing her, she had probably overloaded you with information and that when you thought to call, you figured it was too late. Then, he apologized for making me come for nothing and thanked me for my efforts to cover you. He didn't look happy at all." Then, flashing a smile that had been contained for a while, José added, "I see he made you pay dearly for your escapade."

"You think he's that mad at me?"

"No, I don't. I'm convinced he's already forgiven you. He was just upset and disappointed. Besides, it's obvious you've already made your act of contrition. It shows. Also, so as not to worry him further, if I were you, I wouldn't tell him about your meeting with David, nor about the CUC."

"So, you knew about it?"

"Yes, I knew the organization wanted to approach you, even though I didn't necessarily agree. It was not my decision. Most humanitarian workers come on mission for two or three years and then return home. I believe that their testimony on what is happening on the ground can help us in the mid to long term by informing the international community, but I don't agree that they should be directly involved in our political actions... And frankly, what I don't like most about this is that your dedication and unbridled enthusiasm could cloud your judgment. Besides, you'll be my responsibility... So, I advise you to follow my instructions carefully or you will regret Father John's punishments."

After these last words, an awkward silence suddenly reigned in the room. Attempting to create a diversion, José turned to look at the photos taped on the wall above the desk. When his eyes fell on the one showing Francis, Paul's brother, he noticed the family resemblance.

"Is he your brother?"

Paul simply nodded and kept silent.

"He looks like you; a little older, maybe?"

"Yes, that's my brother Francis... Was my twin brother. As you've noticed, we're not identical. It's special that you say he looks older because he came first. This picture was taken a few months before he passed away, two years ago."

"I'm sorry," José said before turning to the photo again. "What happened?"

"He took his own life."

José looked down, a little embarrassed by the intensity of Paul's gaze, and said, almost in a whisper, "He must have been very unhappy and desperate."

"Surely, but it did not show. I always thought we had a kind of osmotic relationship. Throughout our elementary and high school years, he was always there to protect me. Afterwards, I realized he never really confided in me. He was my protector. So, I think he made sure I did not detect any sign of weakness in him. I didn't see it coming, and I lost ground for a while."

"Then he let himself be trapped by his own misfortune," José said thoughtfully. "He must have been consumed from the inside by feelings too long repressed, slowly at first, and then unconsciously, to maintain this image of strength on which others could rely. I think that hidden feelings, accumulated over the years, can develop like a nasty stomach ulcer; and when it bursts, the pain becomes so great that we lose all self-possession. We just want to extinguish the fire burning inside us."

Paul nodded slowly two or three times, pondering on José's explanation.

"It must have been difficult for your parents... And now they must be worried about you since you left."

"Oh, they weren't exactly happy to see me go, but I think they understood what I was doing even if they didn't necessarily agree. I needed to take a step back," Paul replied with a slight doubt in his voice as if trying to convince himself.

"And you signed a two-year contract as a lay missionary in Guatemala. Quite a setback if you ask me."

Paul remained silent, staring at José with a glint of mistrust in his eyes.

"But you seem happy here," José added. (Then, smiling again) "Maybe not today, but most of the time."

"I needed to give a new direction to my life," Paul

confessed. "And to be here helping you to the best of my knowledge is what enables me grow humanly and spiritually. I feel alive again. You see, I believe that you and your people have reached a level of maturity towards life, towards death, that most people don't even suspect. And I think that those who try to put you down and want to hurt you are being immature."

"That's all well and good, but that doesn't mean you have to agree to work with the CUC."

"Why not?"

José eyed him severely, frowning for a second or two before giving up.

Resigned, he added, "Okay. Now, listen! We are organizing a leaflet distribution in Chimaltenango for next Sunday. If you can come you will meet some leaders of cooperatives that you may have to visit regularly as part of the work that you will have to do in replacement of Eduardo and get a better idea of what we do at the CUC. Jim Coulter, one of your colleagues working in another parish, will join our group."

"I know him well. We attended the same training workshop in preparation for our venue in Guatemala."

"It's always people from outside the target area who hand out flyers. The locals would be too exposed. In return, they must be prepared to create a diversion if things go wrong somehow."

"You are being cautious."

"Distributing leaflets can be a very hazardous activity in Guatemala."

"I'll come."

José nodded. "Okay then. Well, I must go now. Get some rest!"

José stood up, put the chair back under the desk, and taking advantage of the fact that he had his back turned to Paul, he took out a cigar of the inside pocket of his jacket before turning around and handing it to Paul.

"Here's a little gift to make you forget the Padre's punishment."

Baffled, Paul automatically grabbed the cigar and, scanning José's laughing eyes, guessed the meaning of the gift.

"Anna gave birth!"

"Last night. I am now the father of a beautiful little boy. It went very well, and Anna seems to be recovering faster than I thought. You can come see the baby anytime."

Paul raised his cigar in victory. "It's great news! I'm so glad for you both."

José waved him off and walked out.

Chimaltenango

On the day of the leafleting operation in Chimaltenango, too excited to participate in this new adventure, Paul was up well before dawn. When he left the rectory to go to the rallying point, the village was slowly emerging from the torpor of the night, with veils of mist still lingering. Roosters began to crow and soon the dull hum of a bus engine could be heard approaching from a distance. Paul joined José and a few others who were already waiting outside the medical clinic. They nodded to each other, wishing "*Buenos Dias.*" Most had a puffy face due to lack of sleep.

José was finishing giving instructions to his group when a yellow school bus pulled into the square and stopped in front of the clinic without turning off the engine. José had to raise his voice to be heard.

"Upon arriving in Chimaltenango, we will disperse into the public square to mingle with the crowd for a few minutes before heading to the church to join the participants in the operation coming from other regions. The meeting will take place in the basement of the church. That's where we'll be given the leaflets to distribute. We will then work in pairs."

While talking, José occasionally glanced at the few passengers getting off the bus to stretch their legs. He finally nodded kindly to a passenger who was about to step off. He then turned to Paul and motioned for him to look toward the bus.

"Here comes your friend Coulter."

The latter presented an oblong face with a naturally tanned complexion. Unconsciously, Paul and Gendron had dressed in the same way, except for the headgear. They both wore a pale T-shirt under a light-brown worn-out jacket, jeans, and sneakers. Paul had his straw hat on while Gendron covered himself with a cap. Sunglasses protruding from the front pocket of their jacket and a camera slung over one shoulder completed their outfit. Everyone else smiled and relaxed at the sight of the gringos dressed as common tourists.

Coulter first shook hands with José and then turned to Paul.

"Hi Paul, I'm sure glad to see you here!"

Paul looked at him with a playful glint in his eyes.

"Well! Dressed as we are, if we travel together, we'll look like the Thomson and Thompson detective twins in the *Adventures of Tintin*. All eyes will be on us."

Both laughed heartily, while José looked at them with a raised eyebrow, suspecting an insider joke.

Noticing the question mark in José's face, Paul said, "Don't tell me you've never read or even heard of the *Adventures of Tintin*?"

José shrugged and shook his head no.

"Tintin is a very popular comic strip character in the French-speaking world, in which the Thomson and Thompson are twin detectives who are a little bit clumsy, always dressed in a folkloric way, thinking they will go unnoticed, but who are seen as a big pimple on the nose precisely because of their disguise and their resemblance. Only their moustaches distinguish them," explained Paul.

Acting as if he were outraged, Coulter said, "It is most likely that the sixth album of the Adventures of Tintin, *The Broken Ear*, has been blacklisted in Guatemala and most of Central and South American countries."

Both laughed again, and José was delighted with their good mood.

Then, seeing that the others had started to get back on the bus, Coulter became serious again.

"José, the committee has suggested that Paul and I participate in the operation only as observers. This would give Paul a good opportunity to see how we operate. We will take pictures as if we were tourists. It may also help us evaluate the effectiveness of the operation."

"Great idea!" José agreed, clearly relieved not having to worry about Paul anymore.

They were the last to board the bus, which left immediately, spewing thick black smoke as usual.

Despite the deafening noise caused by the bus engine and the jolts felt on the bumpy secondary road they had taken to avoid attracting attention, most of the passengers were trying to recover from a shortened night's sleep. It was almost impossible to have a conversation; only the cries of frightened chickens that a few peasants carried in wooden cages to sell at the market in Chimaltenango managed to break through the racket sounds.

José was sitting at the front of the bus next to an old Mayan native woman, while Paul and Coulter sat side by side in the second to last row where they seemed to have fallen into a comatose state, almost. The rare signs of activity that could be observed from the two gringos were when they were mechanically waving their arms to push away the few feathers flying in front of them. The rest of the group from Concepción had scattered around, mingling with the other passengers.

To reach the large market square, their bus had to slalom between dozens of other buses that miraculously managed to avoid each other and the many people in the surrounding streets. They ended up parking at the end of a row of other buses double-parked on the street along the north side of the *Parque Central*. The public park was at least ten times larger than the Concepción one and had become for the day a crisscrossing maze of erected back-to-back peasant shops. Even though it was still early in the morning, the square was already swarming with hundreds of natives from various Mayan communities, creating an impressive mosaic of exotic colors.

Suddenly, several army trucks rolled in from all sides, causing widespread panic in the market square and surrounding streets. People started screaming and running around as the soldiers emerged from the tarpaulin-covered trucks like swarms of angry bees coming out of their hives.

As their bus emptied, Paul and Gendron stood by their window and watched helplessly as the crowd panicked. Outside, soldiers were trying to block all the exits from the park while others were conducting identity checks among those trapped in. José, who had been standing at the front of the bus, giving further instructions to the members of their group as they exited, finally noticed the passive attitude of the two lay missionaries still glued to their seats. He shouted at them to move.

"Paul! Jim! Hurry up!"

They jumped on their feet and joined him.

"As you may have guessed, the operation is cancelled. We came across a military operation. But it's probably a coincidence, because otherwise they would have waited until we have started to distribute the leaflets. In any case, it seems to be a simple identity check as they have been doing randomly for some time now. They will arrest anyone whose papers are not in order. Okay, here's what you're going to do: mingle with the crowd, make yourself visible, you're not at risk. They'll see you as tourists. And that might dampen their spirits. These raids never take place during the tourist season. Are you okay with that?"

Both nodded yes.

"Perfect! We'll meet in the church, say, in 30 minutes at the latest." He could see in their eyes they were ready. "Go now!"

With the command vehicle parked in front of the terminal at an angle to the Concepción group's bus, the commanding officer was watching his unit's deployment with a carnivorous smile when he saw what looked like two gringo tourists with cameras getting off a bus. He frowned and his smile immediately turned into a grimace. He did not want to see tourists appear like that in the middle of his military operation. He called out to a sergeant who was giving orders to a small group of soldiers. The latter turned to see his commander beckoning him to approach and look in the direction of Paul and Coulter, who had just stopped to observe two soldiers bluntly interrogating two teenagers.

"Get the word out. I don't want to see any excessive use of force."

"Aye, aye, sir," replied the sergeant. He gave the military salute and hastened to spread the message.

The commander then moved on toward the two aid workers, whose presence had already attracted a crowd of adults protesting vigorously against the soldiers' behavior.

Coulter's eyes, who had been watching the scene silently with a quizzical look, trying to clear up an impression of déjà vu, suddenly lit up.

"Damn it, Paul, I recognize them. Camillo and Philipino. They are from my region... We can't let this happen."

"Let's try to intercede for them by pretending they came with us as tour guides."

Before they could act, they heard an authoritative, though not aggressive, voice calling out to them from behind.

"*Buenos días, señores.*"

Paul and Coulter turned abruptly to find themselves facing the commander, who was staring at them with a forced smile under cold, gray eyes. Becoming aware of the presence of the commander, the people who were protesting the arrest of the youngsters fell silent. With a slight movement of the head, the commander ordered the soldiers to take the youths away. Then he turned his attention back to the two lay missionaries.

"I am Commander Fuentes, the officer in charge of this operation."

Paul and Coulter remained silent even though it was obvious that the commander was inviting them to introduce themselves.

"I'm sorry you guys showed up in the middle of our operation. We were told that communist rebels would come to mingle with the crowd and try to corrupt them. We had no choice but to intervene to protect the population and prevent possible terrorist attacks," the commander said.

"We thank you commander for these clarifications, but we

are very concerned about what is happening to these two young boys we hired as guides and that your men have apprehended," Coulter said, pointing to the youths who were being taken to a military truck.

"Look, my men may have made a mistake. But there is nothing more I can do here to correct the situation. You will have to follow me to the Military Commissariat Office if you want to intercede on their behalf."

While the commander was offering a solution to the problem that sounded more like a challenge to them, Paul and Coulter had their eyes on the military truck leaving the place. They briefly looked at each other to consult and finally accepted to go with Fuentes.

Upon their arrival at the commander's office, Paul and Coulter quickly realized that the cordiality the commander had showed them at the public square was not genuine. Fuentes did not invite them to sit, so they remained standing as the commander was meticulously examining their passports and work visas.

After a moment of heavy silence, he ended up mumbling without looking at them, "*Misioneros eh!*"

Then he handed them their papers, looking at them suspiciously and disdainfully.

"What are the names of these two youngsters again?"

"Camillo Rodriguez and Philipino Sanchez," Coulter answered.

"They didn't have their identity papers with them," Fuentes added.

"Yes, but as you just said, they are teenagers, and they certainly didn't expect to have to show any identification,"

Coulter replied.

Still staring at them, Fuentes ordered the soldier posted to guard the door of his office to bring the boys.

Having succeeded in freeing the two teenagers, Paul and Coulter ended up getting to Santa Anna church, but an hour later than the time set by José to join the others. Compared with the chaotic situation caused by the military intervention at the public square, things were calm around the imposing white stucco building, flanked by two large towers. Except for the many lit candles, placed directly on the floor on each side behind the benches of the central aisle, it was quite dark inside the nave. Only a few women were kneeling on the floor behind the benches of the left side aisle, praying before lit candles. Just to the side, along the wall to the left, a life-size grotesque mannequin, depicting Christ with his head crowned with thorns and dressed in a long purple tunic, stood behind the glass façade of a large wooden box.

Sitting on a bench further down the left side aisle, José was regularly casting nervous glances towards the vestibule. As the main door opened, a stream of light made its way to the middle of the central aisle, but José could only catch a glimpse of two silhouettes crossing the threshold. Since he did not want to attract attention, he got down on his knees, pretending to pray, hoping that they were the two aid workers.

When Paul and Coulter slid onto José's bench, the latter cast an irritated glance at them and asked in a low voice, "For God's sake, where have you been all this time?"

"We helped free two young people from my region. Soldiers arrested them right in front of us," Coulter replied in a muffled voice.

"Okay, now I want you to wait here for a few minutes before joining me in the backyard."

José got out of the bench, walked up to the balustrade, in front of which he took the time to genuflect and sign himself, before disappearing through a door hidden behind a column to the left. After watching him do so, Paul, perplexed, turned to Coulter.

"I don't get it. He really doesn't look happy."

Coulter signaled to stay silent. Paul refrained himself, and for the rest of their waiting period, he kept his gaze fixed on a large wooden crucifix hooked on the wall behind the altar.

Hiding in the doorway of an exterior stone staircase leading to the roof of the church, José waited for Paul and Coulter to come out. Six other members of the Concepción group and a newcomer were all seated, leaning against the five-foot-high stone wall surrounding the church's backyard. They stayed crouched in a heavy silence so as not to be seen or heard from the street running along the wall, praying that the old green van parked inside the compound would not attract attention.

As soon as the two stragglers opened the exit door, José signaled them to shut up and duck down to join the others along the wall. He then went up on the roof to get an overview of the situation and to check if the way was clear.

He walked in a crouched position to the front of the church where he could see that the military operation was still going on in the public square and the surrounding streets. He got down on all fours as military trucks drove past the church but kept his head up high enough to see that the backs of the trucks were filled with people who had been arrested, flanked by soldiers. While following the course of the trucks on his right, he noticed that three soldiers were posted at the intersection of the street in front of the church and the one running along the wall behind which his group was waiting.

Then his attention was drawn even further to his right by an old white van slowly driving up a deserted street leading directly to the square. Intrigued by the incongruity of the situation, José couldn't help but follow the course of the vehicle, with the impression of witnessing a scene in slow motion. Once at a few hundred feet from the square, the van suddenly stopped right in the middle of the street. Two men rushed out of it and ran away. A few seconds later, the van exploded and turned into a fireball, causing a new wave of panic in the public square. Surprised, the soldiers were slow to react and the people who had been trapped in took the opportunity to flee. José looked back at the intersection where the three soldiers had been posted. They had disappeared.

The members of José's group had heard the explosion and were staring anxiously at the entrance of the stairwell, wondering what could be going on. José quickly emerged and urged them to get into the van parked in the backyard. The explosion had offered them a way out.

They left the city, away from the hustle and bustle, and headed down a winding dirt road through an area of bare mountains about ten miles to the east. Except for the newcomer, who turned out to be the driver, all members of the group sat on benches installed on either side at the back of the van. Coulter was sitting next to Paul, and José directly opposite Paul. For a while, everyone remained on the alert or lost in thought. It was only after having reached the mountainous region that they could look at each other and express their relief with smiles. Yet José still looked upset, and even more so when he had to listen to Coulter explain how he and Paul had managed to free the two young boys.

"... After having succeeded in getting safe-conducts signed by Commander Fuentes, we accompanied them to the bus terminal, bought them tickets and made them promise to wait patiently inside for the next departure for their village," Coulter concluded with a wide smile of satisfaction.

For his part, Paul was truly flabbergasted by José's cold attitude towards them. And indeed, the latter could not contain himself any longer.

"Don't you understand how you put the whole group at risk by making us wait for you while the soldiers checked everyone's identity, probably trying to get hold of people like us. The other groups had left town long before the soldiers had finished deploying. Someone must have suspected that we were stuck at the church and managed to create a diversion to allow us to escape. What you've done to free Camillo and Philipino was a good action, but in doing so you have put all of us at undue risk. You cannot act as if you still were in your country."

Paul had had enough of this paternalistic talk. His eyes flashed with anger, and when he began to answer José, everyone was surprised by his decisive tone and held their breath in anticipation of what was to come.

"Listen José, I know very well where we are and, despite what you think, I still believe that we did the right thing. We have managed to free these two boys and we were the only ones who could do it. Then, since we weren't coming, you didn't have to wait for us. If you hadn't been in the church, Jim knew where you were supposed to go and what to do."

Hearing that last part, José glanced at Coulter, who bowed

his head in shame. Paul continued to make his point with a more moderate and conciliatory tone.

"You know, I'm old enough to be capable of weighing the pros and cons of a situation and make a responsible decision."

All eyes turned to José, apprehensive about how he would handle Paul's objection. Instead of reacting immediately, José took a moment to reflect on what Paul had said. Then he looked at Paul again, this time with gentleness in his eyes.

"I'm sorry, Paul; please forgive me. (Then smiling) Now I see that you've become a true *compañero*!"

Paul understood the value of the appellation; it freed him of the tension created by this sudden confrontation between him and his friend. Relieved, they shook hands in the manner of the wrist wrestlers.

Paul's eyes brightened and he repeated in a vibrant voice, "*Sí, sí, compañero!*"

All the others, except Coulter, too surprised by this sudden shift, cried out in unison, "*Sí, sí, compañero!*"

Shortly after the argument between the two friends had ended to everyone's satisfaction, the van driver glanced in the rearview mirror and announced that they were arriving at their destination. Seconds later, the van made a right turn and began to ascend a steep and rutted sandy trail winding up the side of a hill. The ride seemed quite long for the passengers seated in the back who were struggling to stay on their wooden benches. Eventually they came to a small plateau hidden behind a ridge at the top of the hill, where two more vans were parked next to a small wooden hut with a tin roof.

David and fourteen other people, including three Ladino women, came out of the shack to welcome them. The van stopped behind one of the other two vehicles and everyone got out with a big smile of relief, happy to be able to set foot on flat, stable ground again. They shook hands and hugged each other. A little away from the others, David started questioning José.

"We were getting pretty worried. We have been awaiting your arrival for almost three hours. When we came in sight of Chimaltenango, our group and the other one realized that the army was in town, so we decided to abort the operation and come here as planned in case something went wrong. What happened?"

"Since we came from the north, that's probably why we didn't see the military coming. We were still looking for a place to park when they appeared in the public square. I then asked the members of my group to disperse before regrouping in the church. Some of them had to show their identity papers, and Paul and Coulter were summoned for questioning by the commander of the military operation." Then, seeing the latter heading towards them, José said, "I'll explain later."

David left them and went to meet the driver of José's group, who was preparing to move the van alongside the other vehicles. David beckoned him to wait.

"You sure you've not been followed?"

"I didn't see anyone on the road. It was empty, and no dust clouds appeared behind us."

"Okay then, but you know you can never be too careful. So you will now return slowly to Chimaltenango, have a look around, and see how the situation has evolved in town. Tomorrow morning, at daybreak if you're not back yet, we'll go to another shelter. Good luck!"

By nightfall, most had already gone to bed, fully dressed,

under wool blankets on the dirt floor. Paul and Coulter were settled in a corner with wool ponchos that had been lent to them. An oil lamp dimly lit the interior of the shack. Low heat was radiating from a small wood-burning stove installed in the center of the single room. Someone dimmed the lamp to a mere glow. David and José, both wrapped in a blanket, went out to take the first night watch.

They walked away from the shack and leaned against a ledge near the steep path they had taken. From there, they could distinguish the road at the bottom of the hill and had a spectacular view of the starry sky.

For now, the road seemed empty, although they could only see its layout, which appeared clearer than its immediate surroundings. After a satisfied look at the dark mass that the shack had become, David offered José a cigarette. The latter lit it, then brought out a bottle of aguardiente and handed it to David.

"Thanks, it's pretty cold tonight." While José was scanning the night towards the road, David took a big swig of eau-de-vie and let out a heartfelt "Whew" after gulping down his sip. He took a deep breath and handed the bottle to José, adding, "It really warms us, but if we drink too much of it, we'll start to see things that aren't there."

José put the bottle back in its hiding place and the two remained silent for a while looking at the stars until David broke it by sharing what was on his mind.

"When I think that your ancestors could interpret the language of the stars... Sometimes I feel like I'm living in the middle of a long period of obscurantism and regression, during which the worst instincts of people are aroused... Tell me José, are there still astrological priests among your people?"

"There are still a few. Some shamans are too, but they don't show it. They don't want to be identified as such."

Suddenly they heard what sounded like truck engines echoing through the night. They put out their cigarettes, looked behind to make sure there wasn't any light showing from the cabin, and waited in silence. They then saw headlights of at least three large vehicles heading at high speed in their direction. David quickly realized they would stay on the main road.

"It's not for us; they're driving too fast."

But when the vehicles had disappeared from their sight, they still held their breath and strained their ears in case the mini convoy would stop a little farther away, out of earshot, to come back and look at the trail taken earlier by José's group and see where it might lead. After several minutes of tension, they looked at each other, relieved, and began to breathe normally again.

"It's quite odd that they decided to carry out such an operation today," José said, thinking aloud. "Maybe they put on a show to hide that they were looking for specific people. They wanted to check everyone's papers."

David followed up saying, "Given the critical situation prevailing on the west coast because of the strike in banana plantations, we must be even more careful than we have been so far. I think it's best to cancel the operations planned for the next few weeks."

Inside the shack, Paul and Coulter were sleeping soundly under the pale glow of the moon filtering through the only window near which they had settled for the night.

David walked silently towards them, being careful not to

awaken the others. He first awoke Paul by shaking his shoulder slightly. The latter opened his eyes almost immediately on David's face giving him a warning look with a finger on his lips to keep quiet. Paul understood it was their turn to ensure the night watch.

José smiled when he saw Paul leave the shack, followed by Coulter who, still numb from sleep, threw a "brrr" as tightening his poncho around his neck and shoulders. He handed them the blankets that had kept him and David warm.

"Sleep well?"

"You're kidding me? I feel like I slept for five minutes," Coulter replied sarcastically, with billows of breath steam coming out of his mouth. "And it's so cold that there is no risk that we fall asleep during our watch."

Paul looked up at the sky and said, "And the sight is grandiose. Three hours will pass in the blink of an eye."

Before leaving, José offered them what was left of the bottle of aguardiente.

"Here, there's enough left to warm you up."

Coulter took the bottle, and without further ado drank a good shot and choked, triggering bursts of liberating laughter from the other two.

"It's burning like hell," Coulter ended up saying in a hoarse voice and watery eyes. "I've often seen natives drink it when they carry loads up the mountain, but I didn't think it was this strong. I understand its usefulness even more now."

In his turn, avoiding acting thirsty, Paul took a tiny sip.

"Whoa, that's a real kick! (Then, looking at José) I was impressed with the way the situation was handled in Chimaltenango—the diversion, this hiding place..."

"There's always backup plan. We do have flaws, though. For

example, we can't predict the army roundups used for recruitment. This one was out of the ordinary. I was expecting a diversion, but I wasn't aware of the details. I was as surprised as you."

"The commander who challenged us in the public square mentioned the presence of rebel elements in the area," Coulter recalled.

"David and I have debated the question, but the more I think about it, the less I believe they were coming for us. During our watch, we saw three armored vehicles pass by that seemed to come from Chimaltenango. I don't think they would use armored vehicles against us if they were after us. But they might have information about guerrilla movements that we don't have. Anyway, we decided to postpone our next interventions for a while."

Surprised to hear what José had just said about the guerrillas, Paul asked, "So the rumor going around about the presence of communist rebels is true?"

Looking into the distance, José frowned.

"There is a group called ORPA, for 'Revolutionary Organization of People in Arms', but as far as I know, its members are hiding in the Peten jungle. You must also keep in mind that the Guatemalan governments have been known to use the communist threat in our recent history to justify the atrocities committed by the army and paramilitary groups, and to get U.S. military assistance...

... When the Spaniards arrived at the end of the 15th century, they said we were not human, thus giving themselves a clear conscience to kill us and steal our land. In their view, we were pagans. Then after being converted to Catholicism, we became beasts of burden. And now they call us communists.

Any name that justifies the massacre of our people and land grabbing is good for them... If we lose our land, we will also lose our soul. Our culture survives in the *milpas*."

José paused and looked them in the eyes, making sure he had their full attention before continuing.

"And don't be fooled, what you are doing here as lay missionaries and missionary priests is regarded by some generals as subversive as communist activities."

Coulter felt José was pushing the note a bit too much and said, "And so, we might as well say that Jesus would be considered a communist revolutionary if he were living today."

"Perhaps, but don't forget that he did not take up arms and never joined the Zealots," Paul retorted with a smile. Then turning to José, he asked him what he thought of the guerilla movement.

José became thoughtful for some time and then said, "Regularly, cyclically, one could say, for almost five hundred years, there have always been uprisings and guerrilla warfare has always existed. And it did not really change our fate. Personally, I believe much more in the efficiency of peaceful political activities, like what we are doing within the CUC. We denounce, we raise people's awareness, we organize massive resistance like the strike on the Pacific coast, and we try to create solidarity between Mayan ethnic groups and Ladinos who want a country that values equality and social justice for every Guatemalan."

With these last words, José stood up and stretched, staring up into the sky. The others followed his gaze. The full moon, now high in the celestial dome, reigned over the night with its brightness.

"Our people have always had a special relationship with the

stars. And this relationship has always been expressed through all kinds of symbolic signs that form a line of transmission between them and us. (Then, after another moment of solemn silence) I talk too much. I'll try to get some sleep and let you enjoy this peaceful night setting. Be careful with the aguardiente. It can play tricks on you." On his way to the cabin, José turned his head toward them and call out, "Stay alert!"

Coulter watched him walk away after wishing him a good night. Then, looking at Paul to speak to him he held back when seeing Paul's face wet with tears, still staring at the sky.

"What's happening to you my friend?"

"I think I've never felt more alive than I do right now. Here, now, I am conscious of being just a speck of dust in the universe, but I am happy to be part of the great Whole. I am completely at peace with myself."

In the sky, the stars suddenly seemed to twinkle a little more above the dark mass of the volcanoes in the distance.

By mid-morning, David, José, and a few others were gathered around a small table on which a small portable radio was playing a Spanish voice at low volume. Paul and Coulter were still sleeping soundly in their corner. They woke up with a start when they heard the shouts of joy from those listening to the radio. With puffy eyes, they watched, dumbfounded, as the others jumped into each other's arms, claiming victory.

Noticing their dismay, José came to them with a broad smile on his face and sparkling eyes.

"The strike on the coast is over. We have won! The workers not only managed to get a small wage increase, but above all a guarantee of better working conditions and safety. This is important for us because it's the first time we win something using peaceful means. It proves that we can make the government see sense without having to take up arms. It's a great victory for democracy, for our people and our organization."

Paul got up and went to hug him.

A Murderous Trap

A few days later, as the late afternoon sun was slowly coming down behind the mountains west of Concepción, igniting the clouds hovering over the hills surrounding the village, the two officers who had received the revelations from Alfonso the traitor in their office in San Juan, now dressed as Ladino peasants, with their shirts pulled out of their pants, were waiting patiently seated on a cement block at the top of a hill, at the crossroads of two dirt roads, one leading to Concepción, which could be seen in the distance, and the other bypassing the hamlet Tuipoch from behind.

Soon, Jorge and two other youths from Paul's group appeared at the exit of a bend on the Tuipoch road. With the sun in their eyes, the boys did not see the two plainclothes officers until they got close to them. The men stood up and walked towards the three teenagers.

The first officer opened his arms in greeting.

"*Ah, muchachos!* Heaven has sent you!"

At first glance, the boys were clearly suspicious of this unusual encounter. Jorge greeted them and asked what they were doing there.

"We lost control and our pick-up truck got stuck in a small muddy ditch on the road on the other side of the hill not far from here. Do you want to help us get it out?"

"It could be a trap," said one of the boys in *Mam* so as not to be understood by the two men.

"Who are you? What are you doing around here?" Jorge asked again.

The first officer then adopted the attitude of a hunted person, looking around as if he was afraid of being spotted. He hesitated a little, acting as if he would reveal an important secret. He kept his voice down.

"Listen... It is imperative that we get back on the road as soon as possible; we are wanted by the police and the military."

The boys took a step back, ready to run away. Jorge dared to ask why they were wanted.

"We are with the ORPA," replied the second officer.

The first officer immediately told him to shut up.

The boys' eyes glowed with excitement and Jorge said, "Are you guerrillas?"

"We've just came back from the west coast where we helped the banana strikers," lied the first officer.

Addressing his friends again in *Mam*, Jorge said, "Well, if we help them, they may accept to show us their weapons."

From the top of the hill, the boys were able to see part of the back of the pickup truck, supposedly stuck in the mud, emerging from a small ditch hidden by brush on the right side of the road. The officers who were leading the way stopped, and the first officer pointed to the scene.

"See? It's right there. Together, we should be able to get it out without too much difficulty."

They all began to descend toward the pickup. The second officer subtly managed to fall behind the boys. Getting close to the vehicle, the boys began to sense that something was wrong;

the pickup was only slightly tilted. They slowed down their pace. Jorge, who was closest to the vehicle, soon realized that the ditch was not really a ditch anymore and the ground was dry. The front of the pickup was simply hidden by shrubs and brush. A deep sense of despair and apprehension descended upon him. He gave the alarm.

"It's a trap! Run!"

Very quickly the second officer, who had stayed behind them, pulled out a revolver that had been slipped into the waistband of his pants and hidden under his shirt.

Turning around to run away, the youths realized they had been tricked. They froze in place.

"Down on the ground! Hands behind your head," ordered the first officer in an icy tone.

The boys had no choice but to comply. They heard the first officer walk away into the brush and open the door of the driving compartment. Jorge raised his head and saw the man come back with an Uzi submachine gun.

In the early evening, Paul and Father Callaghan had just finished their meal and were silently waiting for Graciela to clear the table. Father Callaghan kept watching her until she disappears into the kitchen. When he heard her begin to wash the dishes, he turned to Paul to continue the discussion from where they had left off.

"According to the bishop, the situation is getting out of hand. The victory of the strikers on the coast has made General Mont's head spin. The military would have destroyed other villages in the north of the country. Then, probably in retaliation, a band of rebels allegedly attacked the Santa Cruz del Quiche military base in the northeast. There were also reportedly ambushes against military patrols in the Huehuetenango region, not far from the border with Mexico. He finally told me that even though the army seemed distraught, it will not last. U.S. military advisers are said to have already arrived in the capital."

He was interrupted again, this time by the sudden arrival of Luis, José's brother, visibly in shock.

"Jorge, Renaldo, and Alonzo—they are dead. They were murdered," Luis cried out before bursting into tears.

Paul and Callaghan leapt to their feet and slowly sat back down, stunned by the tragic news.

"No, no!" cried Paul in despair.

Father Callaghan was the first to react.

"Where is your brother?"

"He has not yet returned from Quetzaltenango. He doesn't know."

"Where are they?"

"They were taken to the public square."

Both missionaries, Graciela, who had emerged from her kitchen upon hearing the news, and Luis rushed outside.

The three bodies had been laid side by side and had not yet been covered with sheets. When they arrived on the scene, Paul stopped abruptly, as if struck by a blow at the sight of the three boys riddled with bullets. He stood there, speechless, feeling dispirited and responsible, his eyes staring at the void like a blind man. Then he approached them slowly, walking like an automaton. In a sense, they were under his care. Some members of the village community were already there, including Jorge's parents, crying silently into each other's arms. Many more were coming now. A mix of cries and moaning began to be heard.

Slightly away from the bodies, Father Callaghan managed to intercept the parents of the other two teenagers and help them as much as possible to overcome the horror and pain about to hit them. He showed himself receptive, compassionate, ready to listen. When one of the mothers collapsed in his arms, he glanced at Paul and saw how downcast the latter looked. His years of dedicated service in countries where such atrocities had taken place gave him an understanding of the distress Paul might be feeling. When friends came to take care of the woman he was supporting, the priest ran to Paul. He grabbed the latter by the arm to take him aside, then placed his hands on the young man's shoulders while looking him straight in the eyes.

"Paul! look at me!"

When Paul's eyes focused on the priest's, the latter said, "Come on, pull yourself together!"

"It's my fault. I got over involved in other projects. I have distanced myself from them. I should have been with them more often. It was my first mission," Paul said with emotion and a tearful voice.

"Look, I too feel partly responsible. And it's normal to feel lost and confused. But you couldn't stop what just happened. Just think, scenes like this are happening all over the country right now. The real culprits are those who killed these youngsters and those who encourage them to commit such crimes. This is not the time to give up, Paul. I need you now!"

The intensity of Father Callaghan's gaze and the truth and power of his words had their effect, and Paul finally nodded slightly.

"Thank you, John. Sorry about that. It won't happen again."

Jorge's Wake

Later that evening, Jorge's house was filled with people who had come to pay their last respects to the deceased during the vigil dedicated to his memory, and to express their condolences and solidarity to the family. Manuel, assisted by José, was about to celebrate a Mayan rite of passage. Both were dressed in traditional costumes consisting of a yellow blouse and flowery pants under a white collarless tunic reaching down to the elbows and knees. The fabric curtain that separated Jorge's room from other parts of the house was now open, allowing everyone to see the body of the deceased lying on his bed. The whole interior of the house was filled with the persistent smell of the chrysanthemums covering the body.

José lit the long candles placed at the four corners of the bed on large wooden holders. Manuel entered the room carrying a steaming cup of coffee which he placed on a small bedside table to the right of the headboard. Then the women, weeping, walked in and came to stand on the left side of the bed. The men stayed in the kitchen, observing in religious silence Manuel and José working around Jorge's body.

Those who stood by the door heard knocking. Since no one was coming in, Jorge's father went to open it to Paul, visibly uncomfortable, hesitating, not daring to come forward uninvited.

"I'm terribly sorry," was all Paul could manage to say.

"Thank you for coming. Jorge liked you very much. Please join us; you are welcome here."

Paul handed him a small paper bag.

"I brought coffee beans and maize grains for his passage into the other world."

Moved by this simple sign of respect for the traditions and beliefs of his people, Jorge's father hugged him. The other men greeted Paul's gesture with a nod.

Light black smoke began to come out of the room with a slight smell of copal. Paul squinted his eyes so as not to miss anything of the ritual. José came out of the room to tell Jorge's father to come to his son and signaled to the others that they could approach. Manuel and Jorge's father knelt in prayer before the body. Paul focused on Jorge's face, whose eyes had been kept open. Manuel began to mutter a ritual prayer in Mam and Spanish, blending names of Christian saints, Mayan gods, and sacred days of the Tzolkin Mayan calendar. His voice being barely audible the mourners fell silent.

"*Aye malaya, Santo Mundo, Santo Silla Bank; aye malaya, Dios del Cielo, estar con hermano Jorge, encontrarse con él con amor. Aye quatro Alcades del Mundo, K-mane, cho, caballero K'oi, caballero Bach, Cuman T'ce, Ik, Noj, Santa Caselara del Mundo, Santa Silla Bank, Santo justicia, da a hermano Jorge los custumbres de las naturales del pueblo.*"

At the end of the prayer, Manuel got up to pour a few drops of coffee on Jorge's lips. Afterwards, he nodded to José, who then began to distribute small, dried, hollowed-out gourds, which he had previously filled with aguardiente, to all the men attending. When everyone had been served, Manuel raised his gourd and said in Spanish, "*Saludos a nuestros antepasados*

[Salute to our ancestors]!"

"We call upon you to welcome our faithful brother Jorge," responded the others.

Everyone emptied their calabash and the women's cries resumed with even more vigor. The men placed their empty container in a bag that José passed around. Once this was done, he left the bag in the kitchen and beckoned Paul to follow him outside the house so they could talk.

"It's good that you came," José said, while closing the door.

"John told me that you strongly suggested it," Paul replied, almost excusing himself.

"I wanted you to attend the traditional wake in tribute to Jorge. This is important for Jorge's parents, for Jorge, and for you."

"I realized it. I felt something like an authentic communion with the others. It gave me a sense of comfort."

"Jorge's spirit is here. I could see it hanging over his body in the room. It will stay a few more days before joining the ancestors," José said with a penetrating gaze.

Paul showed his agreement with this by nodding. José then placed a hand on Paul's right shoulder and his gaze becoming more intense, he added, "We found out who was spying on us. He won't talk anymore. But the situation has become critical for the CUC; since the end of the strike, dozens of people living on the coast with close ties to our organization have disappeared or been killed, probably by death squads. David believes that the ESA, the secret police, is about to work its way up the chain of our organization to Quetzaltenango. So, he decided to join the ORPA and go underground. I don't know about Mireya; I have not yet succeeded in contacting her. I confess that I'm seriously thinking of doing as David did. You see, if they come to suspect that I'm with the CUC, it's not only my family that would be in danger, but all the inhabitants of Concepción. We have to be ready to leave the village and find refuge somewhere in the hills, under the cover of the trees."

Hearing José speak this way surprised Paul and worried him.

"But you have spoken out against the use of violence."

José nodded towards Jorge's house and said, "Yes, that's true. But now Eduardo, Alonzo, Renaldo, and Jorge are dead. Don't you think that's enough? The victory of the strikers has enraged the generals and I think that the government no longer has control of the army. We don't have that much choice anymore. Go into exile or fight. Given his role in the organization, I believe David made the right decision. He is the main conduit of information between all other affiliated groups. He knows too much. If he's caught, our entire organization will be threatened. By going underground, he is protecting us."

"Listen José! I need to take a step back. This is going too fast!"

"I understand. But you should prepare yourself mentally for having to go back to your country. Things can get out of hand very quickly."

Paul had heard enough.

"I'd like to say a last farewell to Jorge before going back to the rectory."

"You could apply a few drops of coffee to his lips. That would surely be appreciated," suggested José.

When they saw José return with Paul to Jorge's bedside, the men fell silent, and the women held back their tears. Paul knelt by the body, mumbled a short prayer, and then, following

José's advice, stood up, dipped two fingers into the cup of cooled coffee and moistened Jorge's lips with it, saying, "Forever, you will stay in my heart." Then he made the sign of the cross and kissed the deceased on the forehead. Whispers of approval echoed all around. Paul kissed Jorge's mother and then walked to the door where the boy's father awaited him. They hugged each other in the Mayan way, on both sides, and Paul left, closing the door.

Traitor's Death

In the middle of the night, Alfonso the traitor was walking nervously through a wooded area on a hill not far from the village, stopping regularly to make sure he wasn't being followed. He went to sit on a stump slightly away from the trail crossing where he was to meet another informant he had recently recruited, and from where he could see anyone coming from all sides before being spotted. The killing of the three young boys had put him on edge and he kept casting worried glances to either side of the paths.

He suddenly straightened up when hearing a creaking sound that seemed to come from further up on the path down the hill. He stood up, on the alert. He listened for the slightest noise until he heard the owl's cry, "Whoo-hoo-ho-o-o."

"Is that you, Emilio? You're late," he said in a strangled voice.

No one answered. Then a strange rustling sound came from behind. Alfonso didn't have time to finish turning around when a heavy object hit him behind his left ear, and everything went black. He was already dead before hitting the ground, face down.

Three men, their faces hidden behind a scarf, stepped out of the shadows and surrounded the body.

"Dirty rotten bastard," a voice said.

The Funeral

The funeral took place the next day on a beautiful sunny afternoon. The inhabitants of the village and the surrounding area had come in such large numbers that the church was filled to the point of overflowing onto the large terrace of the forecourt. Those remaining outside, however, had taken the trouble to respect the interior layout, with the men on the left side and the women and children on the other, leaving a free space in the middle to allow the passage of the funeral procession that was about to begin. A small group of musicians consisting of traditional flute players and a few trumpeters was waiting on the porch.

Inside the church, as the funeral Mass had just ended, the pallbearers lifted the three coffins onto their shoulders. Father Callaghan and his two altar servers, two youths from Paul's group, turned to face the faithful. The priest, dressed in his priestly vestments, with a Mayan shawl draped over his right shoulder, and holding a large white wooden crucifix, went to stand in front of the coffin. Behind him, the altar servers were carrying smaller crosses covered with black cloth. The procession began to advance down the central aisle, moving slowly towards the radiant light flowing in through the open front door. To show their respect and express their support to the victims' families, the members of the assembly stood up as the coffins passed by. Only when he approached the entrance and his eyes adjusted to the changing light could the priest see the large crowd gathering outside.

Once on the porch, he stopped and held up the tall crucifix, which began to glow in the sunlight. The men in the forecourt took off their hats, murmurs were heard, and everyone made the sign of the cross. Father Callaghan looked at the musicians and gave them the signal to start the march of the funeral procession to the cemetery. The band then began to play melancholic music at a slow tempo that harmonized beautifully with the clamor of weeping and lamentations that broke out at the sight of the coffins.

By the time the procession reached the entrance to the cemetery, the sun was already low over the hill facing the village to the west. The musicians stopped playing and stepped aside to let the pallbearers and the rest of the procession pass.

José and Manuel, dressed in the same traditional clothing they wore at Jorge's memorial vigil, were already waiting on a mound of earth near the three small graves in which the bodies of the young boys would soon be buried. The pallbearers came forward and laid the coffins at the edge of each grave. Then they waited patiently for the respective families to gather around their deceased and for Manuel to give them the signal to open the coffins. Only when the sun began to sink behind the hill was it given to them. They then removed the lids from the coffins, exposing the bodies of the three cowardly murdered teenagers, who had been dressed in rectangular wool ponchos called *chamarro*. At the sight of the corpses the laments broke out again with renewed vigor.

Discreetly mingled among the crowd, it was with a tightness in his heart that Paul watched the boys' fathers approach the coffins to place tortillas and vials of *pozol* (a corn-based drink) under the *chamarro*, along with some of their belongings on either side of the bodies. Then Father Callaghan went up on the mound beside Manuel to say a final prayer before the burial.

"Oh, Lord Jesus Christ, as we are about to bury our young brothers, we pray to You, the Savior of our souls and whose Love is stronger than death, so that Alonso, Renaldo and Jorge may rest in peace until You welcome them in Your eternal light. Through Jesus Christ, our Lord. Amen."

And everyone, including José and Manuel, made the sign of the cross with Father Callaghan.

Then the faces turned to the west to watch the last rays of the sun. Soon a crimson-red glow dyed the whole scene. At this point, Father Callaghan approached the coffins and sprinkled them with holy water. Then the pallbearers replaced the lids and nailed them on. It took less than a minute for the darkness of night to set in. Only then did Manuel give the signal to lower the coffins into the graves.

Conciliabule

For the umpteenth time, Paul turned over in his bed, unable to sleep. This time he could not help but glance at his alarm clock. He saw what he didn't want to see: 1:30 in the morning. He could not sleep because his mind was filled with thoughts and images of recent events. José's comments at Jorge's wake that exile or to stay and fight were the only options left tormented him. Unable to bear it any longer, he sighed with discouragement, got up, got dressed and decided to go to the church, hoping to find peace of mind.

Knowing that the double front door remained closed at night, blocked with a large wooden bar, he tried the side door giving access to the sacristy, which, as expected, was unlocked. He found Father Callaghan, alone in the church, kneeling like an ordinary churchgoer before a pew to the left of the central aisle. Only a few prayer lanterns dimly lit the front of the nave. As the priest seemed to be immersed in prayer, Paul remained silent and motionless in the darkness. But the priest had felt someone's presence. He looked up.

"Is that you, Paul?"

"I can't sleep."

"I couldn't either. Please come."

Paul walked over and sat.

"I'm glad to find you here. I need to talk. I'm not sure how to deal with the latest events. What can we do to make things better? What should I do now?" Paul asked.

"You've done well. We have just gone through some difficult times. But we must face the situation as it is. That's why we must speak with one voice and act in concert."

"When I saw the bodies of the boys, I felt guilty and responsible for their death. But more than that, it's in my commitment as a Christian confronted with this savage violence that my confusion lies. I didn't tell you, and I apologize for not doing so, but I got involved in a clandestine group, the CUC, a peaceful movement led by intellectuals sympathetic to the cause of the Mayan and Ladino peasants. They believe that a non-violent protest, based mainly on true information and political pressure, can transform the old colonial mentality and bring peace and social justice to the country."

Getting annoyed on hearing Paul's explanation, Father Callaghan interrupted him, saying, "Paul, I know what the CUC is. I also know that this organization is not authorized nor recognized by government authorities." Then, after letting out an exasperated sigh, he added in a stern tone, "And in addition to putting both you and me in danger, since you are under my authority, I remind you that doing so is not part of your mandate."

"There's nothing to worry about, I just distribute copies of a small newspaper to local leaders as part of my job as co-op representative... But that's not the point. What concerns me most is the fact that I no longer believe the CUC can achieve its goals. It's too late. People are feeling more and more threatened and fear for their families. Even here, some people are talking about active resistance by taking up arms to defend themselves. If that happens, I wonder what we will do."

Father Callaghan took a few seconds to reflect before answering.

"You deserve a straight answer. I'll even give you two: one as a servant of the Church, being part of who I am, and another more personal one. You see, today's Church has come a long way on the path of social action, and I think that's largely due to people like us missionaries, whose work in the field has helped to better understand Christ's social commitment to the poorest and most neglected. Moreover, as you know, this new approach is now presented in the book *Teología de la Liberación* written by the Peruvian priest Gustavo Guttierez, in which he stated that 'Sin may also be of institutional nature. When social, economic, and political structures violate human rights, reducing each other's humanity, or forcing people to live in inhumane conditions, the Church has an obligation to denounce and condemn those structures, and it is the right of the people to alter or abolish them.'

... However, many leaders within the Church fear that this might be a breeding ground for communism. They don't want to give the impression that they are inciting the poor to take up arms and then be accused of destroying social order in a country. Monsignor Urizar was informed by the president himself that missionaries were suspected of being political agitators and that their safety would be compromised. In plain language, this means that our lives are threatened. The president added that he wanted above all to avoid any diplomatic incident. I've been in this situation before and I'm sure we will be repatriated soon. It's a matter of weeks, if not days."

"And we would abandon our friends to their fate after telling them that they have the right to improve their living conditions and that they can demand to be treated with dignity like any other human being?" Paul retorted.

Father Callaghan ignored Paul's comment and went on, raising his voice.

"That being said, if any of my parishioners decide to join the rebel forces, I certainly won't blame them for making that choice, and I'll make sure they know it. But if the Mission Society decides to repatriate us, I will obey. Don't forget that in becoming a priest, I took a vow of obedience. As for you, you should be thinking about your family and loved ones back home. If people in this country decide to take up arms to free themselves, that has nothing to do with your mission. You will have no choice but to return home."

All Hell Breaks Loose

They were suddenly interrupted by insistent knocking on the main door of the church. Paul and Father Callaghan looked at each other, puzzled, wondering who it could be at this late hour. Sensing that something serious might have happened, they hurried to remove the long piece of wood locking the double door. When they opened it, they were surprised to discover several people from the Tuipoch hamlet, led by José, with his mother, wife, and child, waiting outside. José asked if they could spend the night in the church. Father Callaghan accepted at once and stepped aside to invite them in. He then noticed that most of them had left with nothing but their clothes on; only a few had bothered to bring a blanket. He looked questioningly at José, who had stayed with Paul on the other side of the door while the asylum seekers crowded into the vestibule. José came closer to the priest so that he could speak more discreetly.

"I was informed that a group of rebels has launched an assault against the San Juan garrison. When they realized that the rebels had blown up the bridge giving them access to the military base in Quetzaltenango, the military and the police finally gave up and fled down the only road they still had, the dirt road that leads to Tuipoch then to the village. I doubt that in their haste to get to Quetzaltenango they'll take the trouble to cross the village. They'll probably follow the road bypassing it, not to be delayed. But there's still the possibility that they decide to take revenge on the inhabitants of Tuipoch. I've warned everyone, but many preferred to stay put or take refuge in the forest with Manuel."

Father Callaghan then looked at the people still waiting in the vestibule, and said out loud, "Please, make yourselves comfortable as best you can. You are at home here in the house of the Lord."

Then he sent Paul to the rectory with a mandate to bring back any blankets he could find.

José thanked him and was about to join his family, who had already chosen the row of pews where to settle for the night, when the priest grabbed his arm.

"Please José, hold on a minute."

The priest waited for Paul to move away, and then, after placing the wooden spar back in its supports to lock the entrance door, he turned to José and asked, "Tell me, how come you know about what happened in San Juan?"

José realized that he owed the priest an explanation.

"I imagine that Paul has already informed you about the CUC, its organization and activities?"

The priest nodded and José went on, "After the events of the last few weeks, the leaders concluded that they needed to establish contact with the guerrillas. Once this was done, a few CUC members were given radio receivers to ensure that we were fully informed of the guerrillas' actions. I was designated as the contact person for our sector."

Paul was about to open the rectory door when he heard the distant rumble of heavy vehicles, which sounded to him as if they were coming from the heights of Tuipoch. Suspecting that they were the runaways from San Juan, he decided to delay his search for blankets, rushed to the entrance of the courtyard, and waited to see whether the vehicles would enter the village or bypass it.

The humming soon became a roar and the ground beneath Paul's feet began to charge with an unsettling energy. And then it suddenly stopped. But, listening carefully, Paul could still hear the sound of idling engines on stationary vehicles. Time froze for a minute or two. Then he saw a jeep carrying four people appear at the end of the street, moving slowly toward the church. Paul was about to return to the church to warn the others when the jeep pulled over to the side just before the junction with the street running behind the church and leading directly to the public square. The soldier in the front passenger seat got out of the vehicle and began to send visual signals with a flashlight in the opposite direction. The engines of the military trucks immediately began to roar again. The first truck Paul saw approaching turned out to be a troop transport whose tarp had been removed, exposing a dozen soldiers, weapons in hand. As it was getting close to the jeep, the signalman motioned the driver to continue straight towards the church.

Paul felt his throat tighten. Even though the impulse to run to the church to alert the others was strong, he managed to control his urge just enough to see that the second vehicle was getting the signal to turn right onto the street running behind the church. The convoy was splitting in two.

When Paul returned to the church through the side door, everyone inside turned to him, anxiously waiting for him to speak.

Still panting, he took a deep breath and announced in a hoarse voice,

"They're coming... The convoy has split in two. One group will pass in front of the church and the other behind."

Father Callaghan reacted immediately.

"I think it would be wise for all of us to take refuge in the sacristy, away from the front door."

"Good idea!" José agreed. Then, turning to his wife, "Go with Father John. For my part, I'll go up to the roof and see what's going on. Don't move from there until I come to you."

"I'm coming with you," Paul insisted, in a firm and decisive voice.

Seeing the determination in Paul's eyes, José said, "Okay, let's go!"

While the priest was leading the others into the sacristy, Paul and José managed to disappear into the outer stairwell, a split second before the jeep that was driving up the convoy appeared in front of the rectory yard. They had barely stepped onto the roof when they heard three quick honks followed almost immediately by gunfire.

In the sacristy, the refugees remained frozen in an oppressive silence as they listened to the muffled sound of gunfire coming closer and closer, and then the sound of bullets bursting through the main door. Despite the semi-darkness, everyone could see the terror in each other's eyes. Father Callaghan could not help but look through the only window in the sacristy overlooking the street used by the second group of military trucks, just as they were coming up to him. The priest suddenly realized that a soldier had spotted him and was pointing his gun at him. He barely had time to shout, "Everyone down!" when a burst of bullets shattered the window and sent sparks all over the room.

Someone then noticed that Father Callaghan was lying oddly on his left side. He approached the priest, crawling on his hands and knees, and found that the priest was unconscious. He appeared to have been hit in the head and was bleeding profusely.

While this was going on inside the sacristy, Paul and José had reached the roof parapet overlooking the public square. They crouched behind the low wall, just in time to see the lead jeep pull up in front of the medical clinic. In order not to draw attention to themselves, they had decided not to ring the bells, thinking also that the sound of the shooting had already alerted the other inhabitants of the village.

From the roof, they watched apprehensively as the soldier with the flashlight stepped out of the jeep and signaled the first group of military trucks to continue driving toward the northern exit of the village. One of the officers sitting in the back of the jeep stepped out of the vehicle, walked up to the medical clinic, and attempted to look inside through a window. The other officer went to stand next to the signal man. When the last truck of the convoy showed up, he raised his right hand to order the driver to stop and ordered the men out. He then asked two of them to join the first officer in front of the medical clinic and the others to deploy in such a way as to forbid anyone crazy enough to approach them. The first officer then asked the two soldiers who had come to join him to break down the door of the clinic.

Paul and José looked at each other, puzzled, wondering what kind of nasty trick the military had in mind. They didn't have to wait long to find out. The two soldiers who had entered the clinic quickly left to join the others already deployed along the square. The first officer then entered the building. A few seconds later, he rushed out, nodded to the other officer and got back into the jeep. The second officer shouted an order and all the soldiers returned to their vehicle. They left the square without further delay.

The jeep had just turned onto the exit street behind the last troop carrier when an explosion inside the clinic blew most of the facade into the street ahead. A fire broke out almost immediately and spread quickly inside.

Horrified, Paul and José slowly stood up and looked for a moment at the convoy's vehicles, whose headlights had just been turned on as they were about to leave the village. Sporadic gunfire could still be heard in the distance.

"We must put out the fire before it spreads to the adjacent building," José whispered urgently.

They disappeared behind the two big belfry bells and pushed on them until they started ringing.

From the top of the mountain facing the church, the village presented a staggering backdrop, with the fire raging in its center, the tocsin being heard and the taillights of the convoy vehicles moving away in a luminous streak.

A few hesitant people began to appear on the public square, but their encouraging calls quickly prompted everyone around to come out. Soon there was chaos as people began to flock from all sides, gesticulating and unorganized, until José got there and took charge. Some were tasked with fetching buckets to fill from the tap in the courtyard of the co-op building, while others had to set up a long human chain that would bring the water to a dozen men lined up in front of the clinic. The flames licking the black canvas of the night and the faces looking like copper masks evoked a Dantean scene.

Some of those who had sought refuge in the church had taken the injured priest back to his apartment, and Paul had joined them after hearing what happened. Father Callaghan was now lying on his bed with a makeshift bandage around his head. He was sleeping soundly. After examining the wound, which had stopped bleeding, Paul covered the head with a new, more appropriate bandage. Then he turned to Graciela who had remained at the priest's bedside.

"I would like to stay, but I have to take care of the other injured. (Then glancing at the priest) It's not as bad as it looks. But it's a deep scratch that will make him suffer when he wakes up. I'm more concerned about the shock and trauma he suffered."

Paul took a small bottle from a medical kit he carried in the canvas bag slung over his shoulder. He opened it and poured four small white pills into Graciela's outstretched hand.

"Here, take these! If he wakes up before I come back, give him two with water. And then he'll have to stay in bed. Tell him I've gone to see if there are any more wounded."

"Don't worry! I will take good care of the padre," she assured him.

Paul put the bottle of pills back in his bag and left the room.

Graciela placed the pills on the bedside table and then leaned over Callaghan's head to look at the bruise more closely: deep wrinkles between his eyes above the nose showed the severity of the concussion the patient suffered. Graciela tenderly put a hand on the priest's forehead and noted that he had fever. She took a washcloth soaking in a water basin, wrung it out and applied it to the patient's forehead. Then, satisfied, she went to sit in an old upholstered chair in a corner of the room, from which she had a good view on the priest.

What a Waste

As the volunteer firefighters were trying to contain the fire to the clinic building alone, a red pickup truck slowly drove up the church street from the south end of the village with its lights off. It stopped not far from the church on the opposite side of the street. After a few seconds of waiting, two strangers came out of the vehicle. They were dressed like local peasants, with western-style hats pulled down over their foreheads to hide their faces.

They briefly discussed about what they would do, then the driver returned to the vehicle while the other stealthily crossed the street to the hemispherical reliquary monument erected in the center of the church forecourt. By hiding behind it, he could observe what was going on in the public square without fear of being noticed. Seeing that people were still busy putting out the fire, but perhaps not for long, he turned to the pick-up truck and waved to signal the driver to hurry. The latter then got out of the vehicle holding a bouquet of yellow flowers and ran to the entrance of the rectory yard where he stopped, glancing anxiously at his accomplice.

Having received the signal that the way was clear, he moved quickly but cautiously to the presbytery, where he hastened to deposit the bouquet on the doorstep before slipping a white envelope under it. Once this was done, the two henchmen hurried back to their vehicle. They had just climbed into the cab when Paul's motorcycle, returning from his medical inspection tour in the Tuipoch hamlet, appeared at the end of the street. Not wanting to be seen, they crawled into their seats.

Luckily for them, Paul had only one thing in mind, to go to the fire site and see the extent of the damage. He passed quickly without paying attention to the pickup. They immediately straightened up and watched the motorcycle until it disappeared turning right along the north side of the church toward the public square.

"*Vámonos de aquí* [Let's get the hell out of here]!" the man sitting in the passenger seat called out nervously.

Volunteer firefighters had finally succeeded in putting out the fire. Only a few pockets of charred debris were still smoking. The medical clinic was in ruins and the wall and front of the adjacent building were partially destroyed. Exhausted, downcast, looking dazed like zombies, their minds in slow motion, José and the people who had participated in the chore of carrying the water were almost all sitting on benches or on the cemented edge of the square.

This is how Paul found them when he arrived at the scene at the first light of dawn. He slowed down while passing by what was left of the clinic and stopped a little further on. He returned on foot in front of the ruined building. He took off his helmet and stared in disbelief at the damage caused by the explosion and fire. Overwhelmed, he looked down, then turned toward the square as he heard José approaching.

"I've checked! It's a total loss; all the medical equipment and supplies have been destroyed," José told him.

Paul put a hand on his sling bag and said, "Fortunately, we

still keep a first aid kit at the rectory."

"Any casualties?" asked José.

"Only a few wounded, about a dozen. All in the village. Most of the wounds were caused by shards of wood and glass when the soldiers started shooting, before the people understood what was happening. All those who remained in Tuipoch had taken refuge in the forest before the soldiers arrived. They came out when they recognized the sound of my Jawa's two-stroke engine. They are all safe and sound."

Paul hesitated before continuing, and José sensed he had some bad news to deliver.

"What are you not saying?"

"It's John. He looked out of a window when one of the trucks of the second group passed behind the church and the soldiers started shooting. He got hit in the head. At first glance, I would say it's a deep scratch from a bullet. I don't think the injury is serious, but John is showing signs of concussion. He was still unconscious when I left him. Graciela remains at his bedside. We'll have a better idea when he wakes up. But given his age, I'm afraid he won't make it without any physical or psychological after-effects. I wish Mireya were here; she would know what to do."

"I sent somebody to San Juan to ask the guerrillas for medical help. They may have a doctor or paramedics among them," José revealed.

"Well, I'll wait until noon. But, if no one has come by then, I'll take him to the hospital myself... if I can find a vehicle."

"All right! Let's do it that way," José said. Then lingering on Paul's reddened and swollen eyes, he added, "And now try to get some sleep. You can barely open your eyes. If you don't recover, you'll soon become useless. If anything happens, we'll wake you up."

Before continuing, José waited for Paul to nod his agreement.

"In the meantime, there's still a lot to do here and to discuss... many are talking about taking up arms and joining the ORPA. We also need to consider the consequences this could have for the community."

Before leaving, Paul took one last look at the ruins, and let out a sigh, "What a waste!"

It was with a hint of concern in his eyes that José watched Paul ride away on his motorcycle. He then headed to the center of the square where a group of men had begun to actively discuss the situation.

Arriving at the rectory, Paul was surprised and intrigued to see the bouquet of yellow flowers on the doorstep.

"What in the world...?"

He picked up the bouquet, held by a blue ribbon, and saw the envelope hidden underneath. The words "Al sacerdote de Concepción" [To the priest of Concepción] were written on it. For a moment, he was tempted to open it, but in the end, he preferred to wait. It was sealed. He entered and dropped the bouquet and envelope on the dining room table in the priest's apartment, then went to Father Callaghan's room.

When Graciela saw Paul's face in the doorway, she signaled him to be quiet. He walked over to the priest's bed and carefully examined his face. The latter was sleeping soundly and seemed to be getting better; the tension marks on his forehead had disappeared. Paul asked Graciela to join him outside the room. They left the door ajar and talked in low tones.

"He looks much better," Paul said.

"He got restless and muttered something at about four in the morning. I held his hand for a few minutes, and he calmed down. Then I checked if he still had fever. It had gone down. Soon after, he started snoring," Graciela explained.

"This is a good sign. I think he will recover faster than expected. I'm relieved. If you don't mind, I'll try to catch some sleep until noon. It's possible that someone, a doctor, or a qualified medical person, will show up to see him. If that happens and I'm still sleeping, could you please wake me up?"

"You can sleep peaceably, *Señor* Paul."

Somewhat reassured about the priest's health, Paul finally returned to his room. He immediately lay down on his bed, fully dressed. Exhausted, he stayed with his mouth and eyes open for a minute or two, thinking of nothing, sighed deeply and fell asleep.

Repatriation

ater in the morning, a few of Tuipoch's men, including
Manuel the shaman, joined the twenty or so others
already in the middle of the public square in intensive
discussion to decide what to do. After a good while of fruitless
palavers, Manuel raised his arms, thus signaling that he wanted
to speak. All the others fell silent to listen to him.

"I agree with the younger ones. We cannot continue to
receive blows and constantly feel threatened without fighting
back. The traditional calendar of the Long Count tells us that
we will soon enter the era of Baktun 13, under the protection of
the Caban day, which means the beginnings of a new era, a new
golden age for our people. But it also tells us that before getting
there, we will have to undergo the 'test of fire' and make those
who stole our land feel that we will no longer bow down to
them."

José listened religiously to his mentor. He now understood
better the meaning of the ordeal his son Arturo would have to
go through, according to what Manuel had told him during
their journey to the sacred cave. At that very moment, their eyes
met and Manuel nodded as if he knew what was going on in
José's mind. The others reacted positively to the shaman's
harangue. José decided to give practical shape to Manuel's
words.

"There have been reports of massacres in several villages in the north. We must be prepared for any eventuality, even the possibility of having to leave the village quickly. At the very least, we should promptly organize surveillance groups operating day and night, positioned in the hills surrounding the village."

The discussion was suddenly interrupted by the arrival of two pickup trucks rushing into the public square. In the back of each one, eight people, mostly men but also some women, dressed in worn and faded military uniforms, were sitting face to face, four by four, on small wooden benches fixed directly to the body of the vehicles. They all wore red armbands with the acronym ORPA written in white letters around their arms, and a scarf around their necks that they could use to cover their faces. Some of them were equipped with AK 47 assault rifles, most of them with old hunting rifles.

When the vehicles pulled up in front of the clinic remains, was already walking towards them. The other villagers, indecisive or suspicious, preferred to wait in the middle of the square. As José approached the vehicles, he was both surprised and delighted to see Mireya getting out of one of the pick-ups' cabin. She and a man José didn't know came to meet him. Mireya was both very moved to see her friend again and shocked to discover what was left of her clinic. She was speechless. José hugged her. After shedding a few tears, she pulled herself together and introduced the man standing at her side as Carlos, their group leader. They shook hands.

José then turned to Mireya and said, "I certainly did not expect to see you here today. How did you end up with those who attacked the garrison in San Juan?"

"As soon as I heard about the operation against San Juan,

I asked to be part of it as medical support. The ORPA is rather deprived in terms of medical resources. I also wanted to get closer to Concepción and catch up with you guys... Now tell me... How is Paul?"

"I don't really know. I saw him early this morning; he had spent the night tending to the wounded, including Father John... He suffered a head injury, probably by pieces of glass when the soldiers riddled the church with bullets. Apparently, he was looking out of the rear window of the sacristy when it happened. As for Paul, he seemed rather detached to me, considering the circumstances. Afterwards, I thought he looked like someone who had withdrawn into himself. I must say that his eyes were puffy with fatigue. But I'm fearing that something might have broken inside him when he saw the bodies of Jorge, Renaldo, and Alonzo, who were murdered so cowardly."

Mireya gasped in horror. "What? I didn't know."

José looked towards the ruins.

"And then the clinic going up in smoke," José added. "It left us in such a state of confusion and dismay. I didn't pay enough attention when I saw him again this morning. You know, it's a lot in such a short time and we're exhausted."

"I understand. It must have affected him seriously. The death of the boys must have hurt him very badly; he loved them very much. What a terrible news for him! And he must feel responsible. From what you tell me, I have the impression that he managed to suppress his feelings so that he could take care of the injured... Do you know where he is now?"

"He told me he would try to catch some sleep after checking on John."

Carlos decided it was time to intervene. "I'm sorry to interrupt, but I'd like someone to explain to me what happened here."

"Well, I'll leave you to it. I'll try to find Paul and see what can be done for the injured," Mireya said before heading to the presbytery.

Meanwhile, most of the guerrillas had gotten out of the pick-ups to stretch their legs. A few men from the village had approached to inquire about the situation in San Juan. Attracted by the weapons, two teenagers approached two young guerrillas, equipped with old hunting rifles, leaning against one of the vehicles. As they were not much older, the latter proudly welcomed the two boys.

"*Hola chicos!*"

"Is it true that you took San Juan?" asked one of the youngsters.

Wondering if he could talk about the operation, the young rebel to whom the question was addressed hesitated, then turned to an older fighter with a Kalashnikov who had returned to sit in the box of the pickup. The seated man glanced at Carlos, who was still talking with José in the public square. After a few moments, he made up his mind, got off the vehicle, and faced the boys.

"You bet! And it's with these weapons that we were able to succeed," he said, patting his Kalashnikov. Then he removed the magazine and handed the rifle to the boy who had asked about San Juan. Seeing the boy's hesitation, he added, "You can take it. It's not loaded."

While the two youngsters were examining the weapon with awe and respect, some others, fascinated by the assault rifle, joined them.

"With a weapon like this one, you can fire twenty rounds without having to reload. (Then looking at the others) Yep, we took San Juan. And we intend to control the whole area. But even with such guns we will not be able to resist a major attack by the military for long. We are too few; we need reinforcements."

Heartened by the enthusiasm of the teenagers, the fighter had not realized that Carlos and José had stopped talking and were both giving him stern looks.

While this simplistic recruitment attempt was taking place, Mireya was knocking at Paul's bedroom door. Receiving no response, she knocked twice more and opened the door. She found Paul lying fully clothed on his bed, sleeping so soundly that he had not heard. To wake him up, she gently squeezed his left shoulder, while calling to him in a soft, friendly voice, "Paul, Paul, Wake up!"

The latter slowly emerged from his sleep, looking haggard, eyelids still swollen, eyes half closed, dazzled by daylight.

"Uh? Yes? What time is it?"

Then, realizing that Mireya was leaning over him, he smiled blissfully.

"Mireya? But how..."

"Forgive me for waking you like this, and it's almost noon to answer your question."

"What are you doing here?"

"I recently joined the ORPA and was with the group that took San Juan. When I learned that the soldiers of the garrison were fleeing down the road to Concepción, I thought you were at risk of retaliation. I convinced Carlos, the leader of our group, to send a reconnaissance patrol and I asked to be part of it. We were still debating when Gustavo Santiago, who had been sent by José, arrived. Recognizing me, he came over and told us about the clinic... And we came."

Now fully awake, Paul suddenly remembered the events of the night and the seriousness of the situation.

"John was hurt and..."

"I know; José told me. I saw him before coming to you."

"How is he?"

"When I saw him, he was sleeping like a baby. Despite appearances, the wound is rather superficial. I think he's going to recover quickly," she said with a big warm smile to calm him down. You treated him well... and the other injured are fine. They only have minor injuries that can be treated here... I asked Graciela to make some coffee."

Then, seeing two deep folds appear on Paul's forehead, she asked, "You okay?"

"Yes, yes. It's just that the mention of coffee reminded me that there's something I left on the dining table that I need to show you."

"I think I know what this is. Come now; let's talk about it over coffee."

Paul got up with some difficulty, all aching, and went to splash his face with the water from the basin.

In the dining room, a surprise awaited them: Father Callaghan, his head wrapped in a new bandage, sat at the table. The flower bouquet and the envelope that Paul had picked up at the front door were now lying before the priest. The latter had opened the envelope and held the note it contained in one hand.

"I'm glad to see you back on your feet. How are you feeling now?" Paul asked.

"Except for a good headache, I think I'll be fine. Luckily, I have a strong head."

"Did you take the pills I gave you?" Mireya inquired.

"Yes, thank you Mireya; it really works... Well, sit down, we must talk," the priest told them, holding up the note from the envelope.

Then the tireless and devoted Graciela, responding as if to an invisible signal, came out of the kitchen with a tray containing a pot of coffee, a sugar bowl, a small jug of milk and three cups, which she placed on the table.

Father Callaghan then looked at her with grateful eyes.

"Thank you, Graciela! You have done more than enough for me. Now I want you to go and rest."

The priest waited until she had left, then handed the note to Mireya. She and Paul exchanged a serious, concerned look before she began to read the short message. "What does it say?" Paul asked urgently.

"It's a death threat against both you and Father John. It probably comes from the secret police, the ESA. Basically, they call you dirty communists and demand that you leave the country within a week, otherwise you will never see your homeland again."

Knowing that Father Callaghan had already read the threat and had time to think about it, Paul stared at him, waiting for his reaction.

"After reading it, I phoned Monsignor Urizar to inform him of yesterday's attack and the threatening letter. He then told me that other Catholic priests had received similar threats in recent days. In fact, at the time of my call, he was preparing to contact the various missionary societies involved."

The priest paused briefly, then added with a sigh, "We are bound to be repatriated."

"But this is ridiculous and unfair. We shouldn't abandon

our friends when they need us most," Paul protested.

"We'll have no choice but to obey. If we don't, we'll be expelled from Guatemala or even killed. Those who threaten us know who we are and where to find us."

Not yet completely resigned, Paul added, "I hear what you're saying, but my heart tells me to stay."

Mireya then grasped Paul's right hand and looking him straight in the eyes, said, "You have to leave, Paul. If only to bear witness to what is happening here. You won't be any help if you get killed."

Paul remained silent, his torment still reflecting in his eyes.

Back Home

An Emotional Homecoming

December 1980

One week later, Paul was sitting in the passenger seat of his father's pickup truck, on his way back home. They were travelling on US Route 1, heading for Camden. Christmas was only two weeks away. The few houses encountered along the road had merrily decorated Christmas trees on their porches or behind their large front windows. But Paul was not in the mood to celebrate. The weather was cloudy and damp, and he associated the grainy, dirty snow that covered the landscape with the thick, dark veil that clouded his mind. He remained under the impression that he had abandoned his new friends to their fate.

Paul's father was getting more and more concerned about his son's scowl. He could see that he was not at all happy to be back home. Paul had barely said a word during the four-hour trip between Boston and Camden. His father glanced worriedly at his son, who seemed to be hypnotized by the landscape scrolling past the side window.

"We'll be there soon," he announced as he spotted the spire of Our Lady of Good Hope church in the distance, hoping to spark a reaction from his son.

The announcement that they were getting close to the

family farm broke through the emotional numbness that Paul was in. But his father saw only fear and panic in the brief glance his son gave him before returning to stare at the Penobscot Bay, whose salty waters, benefiting from a microclimate, were still free of ice.

Just before entering Camden, they turned left onto the dirt road leading to the farm. They drove past the cemetery where Paul's brother was buried, crossed the old covered bridge over the creek that meandered through the family's land, its water was now flowing under a thin layer of ice, and then, as they came out of a final right-hand bend, the Desilets' farmland suddenly appeared to them in all its extent with the same low hills in the background, except there were no cows in the fields. It was only when he saw the farm buildings that Paul was finally able to pull himself together a bit. He straightened up in his seat, apprehensive about the welcome he would receive.

As they came into the entrance driveway, a small reception committee, including Paul's mother, his sisters, his old friend Richard Lalonde, and Louise, his fiancée, came out of the family home and walked toward them. He barely had time to open his door when his sisters grabbed him and threw themselves around his neck, smothering him with kisses. Then he looked up at his mother, who was waiting nearby, trembling with emotion behind her daughters, too moved to speak. She just opened her arms and he rushed in.

Richard and Louise had stayed a little way away, waiting for Paul to finish with his family. Paul walked up to his friend, who shook his hand while patting his shoulder with the other. Then, and only then, did he dare to look at Louise, who was waiting tensely. She could not hold on any longer, and when he took her in his arms, she collapsed, bursting into tears, and shaking. He managed to stammer out that he was sorry and asked for forgiveness.

Meanwhile in Guatemala

W hile Paul was trying to reconnect with his family without breaking the mood of the Christmas celebrations, the situation in the Quetzaltenango area had quickly escalated. The Guatemalan army had regained control of San Juan, whose garrison had been greatly reinforced. The rebels had retreated northeastward into the region of Santa Cruz del Quiché and the inhabitants of Concepción, feeling more threatened than ever, had taken steps to protect themselves. During the day, they still went to work in the fields, but most of them spent the night in the forest. Shelters of branches and tarps had been set up under the canopy of trees near the pyramid that José and Paul had visited, and which now served as a watchtower. Day and night, a watchman installed in a makeshift cache made with the brush and shrubs that had grown behind the upper terrace of the pyramid, ensured that there were no bad surprises coming from the ground or the sky.

At first light on that chilly December morning, the person who had been appointed to keep watch during the night, emerged from his makeshift shelter with a wool blanket over his shoulders, along with binoculars and a whistle around his neck. He walked to the edge of the terrace on his left to observe the few women and girls who had gone to draw water from the *cenote*. This was consistent with the routine that had been established. He then went to the front of the terrace from where he began to scan the terrain in front of the pyramid by slowly panning left and right with his binoculars. He first focused his attention on the area around a body of water at the foot of the Sierra de los Cuchumatanes in the distance, then scanned the forest back to the bottom of the pyramid. In doing so, he stopped briefly to look through the trees at people bustling around a primitive conical hut and a thatched, wall-less shelter that could be used as a meeting place. On ropes tied to the shelter's uprights, clothes were hung to dry. The watchman ended his round by looking to the right, up the path through the cornfield to the dirt road leading to the lagoon.

After ensuring that the road was clear in both directions, he blew his whistle three times, thus warning those waiting behind the thick grove of trees, which prevented the pyramid from being seen from the road, that they could go and work in their fields. It also signaled to the dozen or so people whose turn it was, that they could engage in a shooting exercise at the site of an ancient Mayan ball game located behind the pyramid.

When he heard the sharp crack of the first shots, the spotter moved to the back of the terrace from where he had a good view over the ruins of the ball game stadium. There, a dozen men lying on their stomachs in the yellowed grass of the playing field were practicing firing at small targets set up along the opposite stand with old hunting rifles. Among them, José was second from left. A guerrilla, proudly wearing the ORPA armband, was slowly walking back and forth behind the group, stopping at times to check the results with small binoculars and encourage the shooters.

Christmas Eve

O n Christmas eve, a light snow falling over the Camden area was twinkling like stars under the outdoor lighting of the Desilets' home. Through the large window of the living room, one could see silhouettes moving in front of an illuminated Christmas tree and hear the muted sound of festive music.

Hearing the doorbell ring, Aunt Maddie, who was standing nearby, peeked into the hallway, just in time to see the newcomers enter.

"Hey, it's Ritchie and Jeanne d'Arc," she announced loudly.

She then looked at the two pre-teens who were desperately trying to disappear behind their parents, so afraid were they of their aunt's pulpy lips, generously buttered with red lipstick.

"Where are my little darlings? Oh, there they are!"

Poor Jamie and Marc—there was no escape from it. As soon as their cheeks were well greased, they rushed to the bathroom to assess the damage and try to make it go away.

In the living room, Louise went to put a new Christmas record on the turntable of an old wooden stereo system, and soon Bing Crosby's "Silent Night" blended in with the hubbub of several people talking at once. Then she scanned the room in the hope of finding Paul, wondering if he had even bothered to show up since he had been rather distant during the last few days, even with her. She feared he might fall back into depression.

The living room was filled with family and friends. Most of them, standing in small groups, glasses in hand, engrossed in conversation. All the seats—including sofas, rocking chairs, easy chairs and even the folding chairs along the walls—were occupied. Paul's sisters were moving among them, offering canapés on trays.

Louise finally spotted Paul leaning against the wall near the entrance to the living room. Despite the frozen smile he managed to maintain for the gallery, he had a fixed and empty gaze, and did not seem to notice what was going on around him. As she was about to cross the living room to join him, a slightly tipsy uncle got up and began to sing "He is born, the Heavenly child" in a powerful baritone voice. Almost everyone stood up to join him. For a moment, Louise lost sight of Paul. By the time she finally got close, he had disappeared. She caught him in the hallway, putting on a winter coat.

"What are you doing?" she asked.

"I need some air. I'm suffocating here. Will you come with me?"

Outside, the snow had stopped falling. The sky had cleared and offered good visibility. The night was cold and the air dry. Louise took Paul's arm and they started walking slowly toward the barn. They remained silent until they stopped to look at the city lights, shining in the distance. After a few tense seconds as each seemed reluctant to break the status quo that had prevailed between them since Paul's return, Louise was the first to speak up.

"I still have difficulty realizing that you are back. We were all worried about you. And after reading the only letter you sent me, I kind of felt adrift and abandoned. Did we still have a future together? And when your mother told me that you were to be repatriated, I thought, 'Thank God, this is finally over.' But now I don't know anymore. Your body is here but not your mind."

Paul listened to her with sadness, knowing full well that he could not really reassure her. And yet, he felt some relief that she was the one to bring up their situation, giving him the opportunity to explain himself.

"You are right, and I am deeply sorry. But I can't help it, I can't stop thinking about my friends in Guatemala, about those youngsters I was responsible for. I left with an aftertaste of an unfinished mission. I feel like I have abandoned them. And now, I really believe that I should be there with them as they go through some tough times."

Louise seemed at first taken aback by the turn the discussion was taking, but when she recovered, her reaction was brutal.

"What? Have you lost your mind!"

"I should be there," Paul repeated with more conviction after clearing his throat.

Louise could see the psychological distress in Paul's eyes, struggling with the depth of his conviction, and she suddenly felt empathy for him.

"You know, deep inside me I feared that something like that would happen. Obviously, we've heard about what was happening in Guatemala. There were even rumors that the country was in danger of falling into civil war. And we hadn't heard from you in a while. I don't know what you've been going through during the last few months you were there, but your attitude since your return tells me that terrible things must have happened."

Then, putting her hands on his shoulders, she added in a softened tone, "You have remained silent, closed up like an oyster. You must wake up now. Get psychological help... You can't go back anyway; the Mission Society would forbid it."

"You're right again. If I choose to go back, it will be on my own."

Shocked to hear this, Louise briskly withdrew her hands and took a step back.

"You are completely off the rails! It doesn't make sense! And then how could your return help them in any way?"

"I am convinced I can be of some help. I can't stay here thinking about them all the time."

"What about your friends here? What about your family? What about us?" Louise asked with tears in her eyes.

Paul hesitated before answering. He felt a lump in his throat and his voice broke when he spoke again.

"I'm really sorry Louise... but I never meant to disrespect you and I apologize if I offended you. How can I explain to you how I feel? During this year I learned to speak a Mayan dialect, I ate tortillas and beans almost daily, I helped these people and felt accepted by them, I was really at ease with their way of life. It was like coming back from the dead. And now that they are really in trouble, I should abandon them to their fate?"

"When you left for Guatemala, I said to myself, 'Paul is going to live with the poor and needy, that's very Christian of him and it should do him good.' But now it sounds like you're willing to die for them. I can't accept that... I think you're the one who needs help the most right now."

With these words, expressed with anger and frustration,

Louise turned away and began to walk toward the house. But after a few steps, she changed her mind, came back to him, and said, "You know that I love and respect you. I don't agree with you, but I'm glad you finally decided to talk to me." Then she kissed him and went home for good this time, leaving Paul baffled.

Later, all these people gathered in the Catholic Church of Camden to attend the midnight mass. Paul sat a bit apart from his family, with Louise at his side. They seemed to have made peace. While most of the faithful present were trying to listen without falling asleep to a homily punctuated by the regular snoring of some, Paul's mind was clearly elsewhere, his gaze lingering first on the details of the Christmas crib before moving along the large wooden crucifix behind the altar to the head crowned with thorns, thus passing in the same movement from the birth to the death of Christ.

As Paul's attention remained on the acceptance of the redemptive suffering expressed on Jesus's face, the ambient sound gradually faded and a succession of images from his journey in Mayan land suddenly arose from his subconscious: his first sight of Father Callaghan's face emerging through a halo of light at the airport; the shy and wondering smile of the young woman on his arrival in Concepción; the indulgent eyes and warm smile of José teaching him the *Mam* dialect in his modest home, under the amused glances of his wife and mother; the Mayan kids hiding behind their mothers' skirts after calling him gringo; Lake Atitlan appearing behind the church of Solola during the motorcycle ride with Mireya, and her face beaming with joy during the Tecum Uman Day in Quetzaltenango. Then the smile that this reminder of happy times had brought to Paul's face faded as these warm images gave way to those of darker times. He saw Eduardo's disfigured face again, the expressionless faces of the three teenagers brutally murdered, the smoking ruins of the clinic, and Jorge's body on his deathbed.

The face of Jesus then reappeared before him, but much closer as in a close-up at the end of a zoom movement, and a quote from the Gospel of John came to his mind: "There's no greater love than to lay down one's life for one's friends" (Jn 15:13). Overcome with emotion, Paul had stopped breathing.

Seeing tears streaming down Paul's cheeks, Louise squeezed his arm to help him come to his senses. When he looked at her, she saw in his eyes that he would not change his mind, that he would return to Guatemala.

Going Underground

An Ambush

On a chilly January night with temperatures around 50 degrees Fahrenheit, a group of seven fighters, including José's younger brother Luis, under José's command, were patrolling an old Mayan pathway still used by people going to the cave near the *cenote* to pray and pay homage to their ancestors, when José suddenly raised his right hand, signaling the others to stop and remain silent. Soon they could hear someone running toward them. José gave the signal to hide in the bushes on either side of the path. As soon as he saw that it was Estéban, their scout coming to report, José showed up.

"Over here Estéban!"

Bent over, hands on knees, Esteban struggled to catch his breath. Still panting, he pointed backward with his right hand.

"A group of soldiers is approaching."

"How many?" José asked.

"I counted six, all armed with machine guns."

"How long before they get here?"

"They move slowly and carefully. I think they'll be here in ten minutes."

José turned to the others who had all come out from their hiding places.

"We can't let them come any closer to our camp. We will

hide again and wait for them. None of them must leave alive."
Then he gave his instructions. "Ubaldo, you will hide a little
further down towards the camp. I'll stand at the other end. The
others, between the two of us, on the same side to avoid hurting
yourself in a crossfire. We'll let them come until they've passed
my position, so that they get caught in the middle. Wait for my
shot before attacking. Ubaldo will take care of the one coming
in front. Even if we only have hunting rifles, we have the
surprise for us. They won't have time to react."

The patrol consisting of a group of five indoctrinated
Mayan youths, led by a Ladino corporal, appeared twelve
minutes later at the end of a bend. They walked in silence,
looking very tense. Realizing that the last one was a native, José
fired a shot in the air before pointing his rifle at him. All the
other rebels fired almost immediately after. By the time the last
soldier turned to face José's rifle barrel, four of the men in his
group, including the corporal, had been shot dead, and the
other, wounded in a shoulder. He dropped his weapon and
raised his hands in surrender.

"Cease fire!" José shouted. "You can come out now!"

Visibly moved and shaken by the violence and speed of the
action, they slowly emerged from their hiding places. Still
aiming his rifle at the last soldier, José told his men to search
the dead ones, grab their weapons and ammunition, and to take
care of the wounded one. He ordered his prisoner to put his
hands behind his back and asked Estéban to tie them up. Once
that was done, he told Estéban to return to his observation post,
in the unlikely event that the group they had intercepted had
come as vanguard.

"What are we going to do with these two?" asked Esteban,
pointing to those who had escaped death.

"We'll try to recruit them," José answered. "After all, they are our brothers. With Manuel's help, I think we'll be able to deprogram them and get them back on the right track."

Then he told the others to strip the bodies of anything useful before hiding them in the bush.

"Cover them with leaves and brush. We will come back later to bury them properly."

Out of the corner of his eye, José saw his younger brother Luis standing motionless in front of a dead soldier.

"What's wrong with you, Luis?"

"*No está bien...*"

"I know, I know... It's never right. But we're at war. Now look at your feet."

Luis looked down at his sneakers. Their soles were tied with ropes.

"You need good boots (then pointing to the soldier's) They should fit you. Take them!"

Border Crossing

As the least crowded place to cross from Mexico to Guatemala, Paul chose to pass through the Cuauhtemoc-La Mesilla border checkpoint, located in a semi-desert area in the southernmost Mexican state of Chihuahua. On a hot sunny day, dressed up simply like a globetrotter with washed-out blue jeans and a plaid flannel shirt, and carrying a backpack, Paul walked across that border with a dozen other backpackers from various Western countries. He had hidden his face behind smoked glasses, a few weeks old beard and a Montreal Expos cap screwed on his head.

A few minutes later, the group had reached the Guatemalan entry point of La Mesilla. Even if its customs officers had the reputation of being laxer than those at the border post of Carmen, more frequented on the Pacific coast, it was still necessary to be accepted by them. However, there was no need to enter the small building. An agent was simply waiting behind a glass counter, overlooking an outdoor gallery where a few Mayas, sitting on a bench, were patiently waiting for the bus going back and forth between Guatemala City and the border.

When the agent asked him to show his passport, Paul handed him a fake ID card with a photo matching his new look.

After a quick glance at it, the agent looked up at Paul.

"You don't have a passport?"

"I'm an American citizen. I thought that wasn't necessary," Paul replied.

"What is the purpose of your stay in Guatemala?"

"I'm touring the Americas. I'm just passing through the country."

"Okay, in that case I will issue you a short-stay visa. I strongly advise you not to hitchhike, because the region is full of bandits. It's better to take the bus."

"Thank you for telling me. I'll follow your advice," Paul said, taking the visa stamped by the customs agent.

Only after he was allowed to enter Guatemala and boarded the bus to the capital did Paul begin to relax. He enjoyed the scenery of the Huehuetenango region scrolling through his passenger window. Someone turned on a transistor radio, and catchy Latino music brightened the atmosphere as they drove along a small river flowing through a deep narrow valley framed by towering mountains, their high peaks disappearing into the clouds. Suddenly, he felt his chest swell with an overflow of powerful emotions and his eyes welled up with tears. Only then was he certain that he had made the right decision. The warmth with which the Natives greeted him as they boarded the bus at each stop comforted him even more in his choice. It gave him the impression they sensed his empathy toward them.

Then the landscape changed, and the viewing field widened, the arid mountains gradually giving way to the lush green wooded hills of the Mayan lands of the province of Quetzaltenango. Getting close to San Juan, they passed a few oncoming army vehicles. The bus had to slow down and make a ten-miles detour when arriving close to the bridge that the guerrillas had blown up when they attacked the San Juan garrison. The bridge deck had been broken at the midspan, with both pieces half-collapsed into the riverbed. Paul was surprised to see that it had not yet been repaired, but even more by the fact that the word 'ORPA' had been painted in large white letters on the exposed part of the deck on the opposite bank. He then realized that the situation had probably worsened.

The bus arrived at the Capital's *Terminal de Autobuses* late in the afternoon during rush hour. The terminal's parking lot was crowded with yellow "chicken buses" and a few conventional coaches, and the place was bustling with people reaching destination or running to catch their bus. A huge black smoke emitted from countless exhaust pipes rose into the sky like a huge cloud of black flies. After finding his way through this maze, Paul hurried to leave the place and the very strong smell of diesel.

He hailed a cab and gave the address - *Pension la Posada, Zona Uno* - where Charles Ramsay lived. Since he worked for the NGO Doctors without Borders and not for a religious organization, Ramsay did not have to leave Guatemala. The cab started at once and headed down *Avenida del Ferrocarri*. As they passed the *Centro Civico*, Paul was impressed by the unrelenting majesty of its sleek, modern administrative buildings, which were heavily guarded by the military. He thought that the Mayas and the peasants were no match for the Guatemalan army and that the rebellion movement was doomed to failure. But he regained hope when, passing in front of the *Biblioteca Nacional* on *Avenida 6a*, he could read on one of its walls "*Cese la represión*" written in large black letter.

Charles Ramsay

When the entrance door of *Pension la Posada*, a small colonial-style family hotel, closed behind him, Paul found himself in a wide corridor at the end of which a reception desk had been set up in front of a staircase leading to the second floor. A plump Ladino woman, giving the impression of being the owner, appeared almost immediately behind the counter. Instead of responding to Paul's "*Buenos tardes*" she examined him from head to toe with a reproving pout, then asked curtly what she could do for him. Paul told her he was coming to see his friend Charles Ramsay. While keeping a suspicious eye on Paul, she phoned Ramsay on an inside line. A few seconds later, Ramsay appeared in the stairs and told the landlady, a glowering Mrs. Ramirez, that it was fine, and thanked her. He walked over to Paul, and they shook hands.

"Hi Paul. Good to see you again. Come up!"

While following Ramsay to his apartment on the second floor, Paul sensed a certain uneasiness on the part of his host, as if the latter was not really pleased to see him. Ramsay only spoke to him again after closing the door of his apartment behind them.

"This is where I live. (Then pointing to the room they were in) There's this large room that serves as a dining and living room, a small kitchen, and a bedroom. The toilet and shower are down the hall."

He invited Paul to put down his backpack and sit on one of the two armchairs placed on either side of the single window at the back of the room.

"You must be exhausted. Please make yourself comfortable. I'll get some refreshments and we'll talk."

As Ramsay disappeared into the kitchen, Paul sat down, still wondering why his coming was bothering the doctor. The latter quickly returned with lemonades and settled into the other chair.

"You did well to call before coming. With your beard, your sunburned face, not to mention your dusty clothes, your Expos cap, and your backpack, you look like a lost hippie. Mrs. Ramirez might as well have called the police if I hadn't been here. If you had called me from the States, I would have tried to talk you out of coming. But since you called from Mexico City... But what on earth did you come here for? And who could have given you my new address and phone number?"

"Jim Coulter with whom you have kept in touch after moving from Escuintla to the capital. And I came back to find my friends from Concepción and try to help them. I couldn't bear the idea of having abandoned them. You stayed. Why couldn't I?"

"Come on Paul, you know very well that I don't work for a religious organization. I have been involved in setting up health clinics, and I was certainly not suspected of being a leftist. That said, however, it's true that certain members of the Guatemalan government do not agree with the way military and police forces behaved. They fear that the bad publicity caused by overt repression will spark condemnation from the international community, which could lead to exclusion and isolation. But they remain suspicious of the Mayas. They believe that the rebels are strongly influenced and supported by Cuban commies. So, they need to work with people they can trust. And since they trust me and I still work with the Mayan population, they told me that I needed protection. But I'm not foolish enough to believe that. They probably hope that I can provide them with sensitive information...

... And that's why I'm now stationed here in the capital, supposedly to assure my security. The downside of this is that when I must go to areas where we have set up medical clinics, two bodyguards follow me in another unmarked car. You see how disconnected they are from reality? How can I get the information they need when people see me arrive with two goons from the regime?"

Ramsay's defensiveness and more reserved tone in giving this lengthy explanation puzzled Paul. He did not want to confront him, so he decided to change the subject.

"Any news from Concepción?"

"I went back there after the army had regained control of the region. I saw what was left of the clinic. I met the mayor and we set about rebuilding it with funds provided by Doctors Without Borders. Unfortunately, half of the villagers have fled to the hills, and some have joined the guerrillas. And I don't think they will return anytime soon because those who joined the ORPA are condemned to exile, their property confiscated and redistributed. As a result, we're short of manpower."

"Any news from Mireya?"

"I haven't heard from her in quite some time. I tried to contact her at her home in Quetzaltenango, but she seems to have disappeared. I wish I could count on her to get the medical clinic back on its feet."

After telling him that the last time he had seen Mireya, she had joined the ORPA, Paul felt the same uneasiness he had sensed between them.

"What are you going to do?" asked Ramsay after a moment of awkward silence.

"I want to find José, the village teacher. I'm thinking of going back to Concepción and then start from there. Maybe someone will be able to give me information and even take me to where he is."

"I hope you understand that you can't stay here. I may be under surveillance... for my protection, as they told me."

"I understand."

"Who knows about your plans?"

"Besides my family, only Coulter and you."

"You are playing a dangerous game, Paul. The military are controlling the area. However, I know that Callaghan's housekeeper is still at the rectory, taking care of the place. You can probably stay there for a few days. In the meantime, you can stay here for the night, but you'll have to leave tomorrow after breakfast. And if someone asks me who came to see me, I'll say that an old friend from the States dropped in to see me before continuing his journey to South America."

Back in Concepción

The taxicab taking Paul back to Concepción left immediately after dropping him off along the public square, near the place where the medical clinic was located. Relying on what Ramsay had said about what had happened in the village, Paul had planned to arrive at nap time to go unnoticed, banking on the fact that no one would be around at that time. He looked at what remained of the health clinic and noted that all debris had been removed and that reconstruction work could begin, as Ramsay had said. Then, seeing no one around, as expected, he calmly headed for the church and rectory.

Along the way, he felt like walking through a ghost town. When he activated the presbytery's doorbell, he looked nervously to the left and right behind him, as it seemed to him that the sound was echoing throughout the village. After a few seconds, he was about to ring again when he heard footsteps coming from inside. Then, the door opened on Graciela who, with frowning eyebrows, wondered who could come at nap time. She froze, a little worried, not recognizing this bearded and smiling man but still looking familiar.

Paul took off his Expos cap.

"Buenos días, Graciela."

Finally, recognizing him, Graciela crossed herself.

"*Santa Madre de Dios, Señor Pooul?*"

"Sorry for the disguise, but I didn't..." Paul stopped there his explanation so much he was surprised by the reaction of Graciela who threw herself into his arms and burst into tears. He hesitated a little, then timidly patted her back. She finally freed him from her embrace and wiped her tears with her apron.

"I am so happy. I thought I would never see you again. Please come, come. Sit at the table. I'll put the kettle on."

"Father John sends his regards and says he prays every day for you and the people of Concepción," Paul said loud enough for her to be heard from the kitchen.

While waiting for the water to boil, Graciela returned to sit with Paul.

"It is not safe to come here. Now, there are police officers on duty all the time watching and protecting the mayor."

"That's why I managed to arrive during the nap. I figured that even the cops had to take a nap. I didn't see anyone. Dr. Ramsay told me what happened after we have been repatriated, and that you were still doing housekeeping at the rectory. I thought this would be the best place to start looking for José and the others who have left. Can you help me?"

"They first set up a camp near the pyramid but then they had to move elsewhere, to a place I don't know. I will inquire discreetly. In the meantime, you can have your old room... but you must promise not to leave the rectory."

Although the kettle had started to whistle, Graciela waited for Paul's consent before going to make coffee.

Paul was asleep, his face dimly lit by the moonlight filtering through the window. A shadow slowly moved toward the bed.

As it began to cover his face, Paul suddenly woke up, staring into the eyes of the intruder who was bending over him. He frowned, trying to remember to whom the familiar face belonged.

The man did "Shhh," putting a finger over his mouth, and then in a low voice, he said, "*Señor Pooul*, I am a cousin of Graciela. I know where to find José the teacher. I can take you to him, but we should leave right away to benefit from the night.

"I recognize you! You are Octavio, and you used to work at the cooperative."

Octavio nodded. Then, to his surprise, Paul lifted his blanket revealing that he had gone to bed fully clothed.

"Graciela told me to get ready to leave quickly. My things are in my backpack," Paul added as he stood up. Then grabbing his backpack, "Ready to go!"

Octavio lifted his own sling bag, smiled, and said, "Thanks to Graciela, she made us food and drink for the road."

They walked up the road leading to Tuipoch, then continued northeast toward the *Sierra de los Cuchumatanes*. Before they could disappear under the forest canopy, which stood out in the distance as a black line, they had to run across an area of open ground under a bright moon. Only once they had reached the forest did they allow themselves to take a break to breathe and quench their thirst.

Octavio looked at Paul who was struggling to catch his breath.

"You okay?"

"Give me... another... minute."

"Okay, but no more. We still have a long way to go and I'd rather avoid traveling in broad daylight."

They set off again, walking briskly on level ground through

a deciduous forest. In the middle of the night, after hardwoods had given way to giant pines, Octavio suddenly raised his hand in a stop sign and crouched down, immediately followed by Paul.

They had reached an intersection with a small logging road. Octavio motioned to Paul to wait while he was going to ensure that it was safe to cross. A few seconds later, he returned and whispered to take cover. Soon they saw a patrol of twelve soldiers passing carelessly on the logging road, making only a casual visual scan. Octavio waited for a few minutes before checking again. Seeing that the way was clear, he crossed over, turned and beckoned Paul to follow him.

They resumed their nightly walk, staying more than ever on the lookout, attentive to the slightest suspicious noise. At dawn, Octavio stopped at a fork in the path and pointed to the narrow side trail down to their left. He told Paul they would take it, but first he wanted to show him something. So, they continued onto the main path, which after a minute or two came to a ledge at the top of a great rock face plunging into a deep ravine whose bottom was still in darkness. Beyond the cliff, on the other side of the ravine, three large grassy mounds of varying heights stood out clearly on open ground.

"These mounds you can see on the other side are all that remained of the ancient Mayan city of Utatlan, the former capital of the Mayan Quiche kingdom, after Alvarado's victory over Tecum Uman's army in 1524. Then the Spaniards dismantled its structures to use them for the construction of the city of Santa Cruz del Quiché, which became the capital of the department of El Quiché and an important base for the Guatemalan army. Our camp is on the other side, a little further away in the forest."

They returned to the fork and took the trail leading to the ravine. The descent becoming steeper and steeper, they had to hold on to the shrubs to keep from slipping. The vegetation at the bottom of the ravine was high enough to hide them from anyone who might be watching from the cliff edge. A narrow pathway leading to the other side had been cut through the grass. The air was so stifling and humid that at the end of the crossing they were literally drenched in sweat from head to toe.

After having quenched his thirst and handed the gourd of water to Octavio, Paul looked up at the rock face and wondered how they would get to the top. When he wanted to ask Octavio, the latter had disappeared. Then he heard Octavio's voice urging him to follow him behind bushes that were hiding an old flight of steps that had been carved into the rock face, that only a trained eye could detect.

Once at the top, Paul could fully appreciate the importance of the ravine as a defensive element. It was impossible for anyone coming from the south to enter Quiché Territory without being seen from the ancient city. Octavio then explained that they would have to go through the open area of the site so that the lookouts hidden in trees at the edge of the forest could see them coming. Once in sight of the forest, Octavio stopped and uttered the owl's cry. Soon after, three similar calls from the forest told them it was safe to approach.

Rebel Camp

José's group had set up their camp in a clearing about 6 miles from the ancient Mayan city. It consisted of about 40 people who could quickly take refuge in shelters made up of large holes dug at the edge of the clearing. Canvases of woven vines mounted on wooden frames and covered with leaves, could be lowered quickly if needed to hide from army search planes or helicopters. They had even built a small henhouse and a few chickens were roaming freely here and there.

In the early morning, José and his family were sitting on logs around a small campfire, getting ready for breakfast, when they heard the repeated call of the owl, relayed to the camp by the lookouts, announcing that someone trustworthy was coming.

"It's probably Octavio returning from Concepción," José told his wife Anna.

Eager to hear from their village, many stood up to greet their comrade. José took his son Arturo in his arms and looked in the direction the call came from.

When Paul appeared in Octavio's wake as they left the woods, everyone looked at him with a puzzled look on their faces, wondering who this bearded man with a blue, white, and red cap was. Paul realized the others could not recognize him with his new look. But he was unable to speak, powerless to repress the emotion that gripped him. He took off his cap. At the same time, Luis, José's brother, coming from another path with two other teenagers from Paul's group, carrying water in plastic jugs, recognized him almost immediately despite the beard.

"*Es Pooul! Es Pooul!*" Luis shouted out. Then the three youths put down their jugs and ran towards Paul.

José handed Arturo to his wife, then quickly approached Octavio while questioning him with his eyes.

"I went to get supplies and fresh news from the village as planned when Graciela came to my parents' house to tell me that Paul was at the rectory and was looking to join us," Octavio explained. Then looking José straight in the eyes, "I thought that you would be happy to see him again."

"You did well, Octavio," José reassured him.

He gave the boys time to reconnect with a good friend they thought they would never see again, before welcoming the surprise guest with a big smile.

"Come Paul. You must be hungry. We were just about to have breakfast. After you have eaten, you will tell me how and why you came back."

Then, turning to the boys, who still couldn't believe that Paul was at their camp, he said, "Hey guys, don't forget that you have to finish your work before you can eat."

José put his arm around Paul's shoulders and led him back to his shelter, where his wife and mother were eagerly awaiting them.

Having eaten, the two friends filled large tin cups with

steaming coffee and walked away from the others. They sat on a log at the edge of the wood and began to talk seriously.

José first wanted to find out how well Paul knew what he was doing.

"So, my friend, you've come back to help in our struggle? Would you then be willing to kill or even risk your life?" he asked, a little sarcastically.

"The last thing I want is to have to touch a gun. As for my life, I place it in the hands of the Lord... And I'm convinced that I can help without having to take a life," Paul replied curtly, vexed by the question, and especially the tone used by José.

"Please don't be offended. I admit that my question was a mischievous one, but I had to ask it. Of course, I knew the answer... and I had something else in mind that might be the option for you, *compañero*," José added with a wink.

Paul accepted the apology with a nod, and said, "I'm all ears."

"All the guerrilla group leaders meet regularly in safe places to coordinate our operations and discuss other issues. At our last meeting, we have discussed the need to set up a network of safe houses outside the combat zones, such as the one we used near Chichicastenango, as well as two or three clandestine hospitals for our wounded. Houses with a large yard protected by a high concrete wall like those found on the hills surrounding Quetzaltenango would be ideal...

... And you see, a gringo like you, with a good cover, could have access to some of the posh neighborhoods, where you can find residences belonging to rich people living outside the country, such as diplomats. Maybe you could rent one for us under a false identity, and continue the work started in Concepción with Mireya."

Hearing Mireya's name, Paul's face lit up.

"Is she still living in Quetzaltenango? Charles Ramsay, the doctor who supervised our work at the clinic, told me that he tried to reach her at her home, but neighbors told him that they hadn't seen her in a while."

"Let's just say that she travels around providing first aid training and treating the injured. However, she still has her home port in Quetzaltenango, but in a different neighborhood and under a different name. You would certainly have to work with her."

"That would be perfect for me... But how are we going to pay for all this?" Paul asked.

"You don't have to worry about that," José replied. "We have benefactors." Before Paul inquired about who these benefactors might be, José added, "I cannot tell you more about that... Well, for now, you'll spend the night here with us. And tomorrow, if you still agree with the plan, someone will lead you to a hideout in Guatemala City, where you will wait quietly for someone knocking at your door. That person will make himself or herself known by calling you by the name of Miguel. It will now be your code name, but not your new identity. This person will explain to you what your cover will be and give you a new ID papers and money. This may take a few days. In the meantime, you will have to stay put and not try to contact anyone. Understood?"

Paul nodded a few times to show that he clearly understood and was not stupid. Then he started to get upset again because José kept his eyes fixed on him without speaking.

"Now what?"

"It's still time to give up and go back to your country. You must understand that by taking this path, you are putting your life in danger. And that is not what I wish for you."

"Thanks José, but I'm determined to continue," Paul immediately replied, still holding his friend's gaze. Then, after winking at him, he added, "I signed up for two years anyway. I still have time to give."

"Very well then," José concluded, although he did not find that last line funny.

At that moment, excited shouts from José's mother and wife drew their attention and allowed them to witness the first steps of Arturo, who had left his grandmother and was bravely advancing, waddling on his legs and flapping his arms, until he reached his mother, who encouraged him by spreading her arms. The two friends greeted the achievement with applause and cheers. When Paul turned back to José to congratulate him, he had time to see the wonder and pride shine briefly in his friend's eyes before the latter became pensive, saying, "I want my son to be able to live in peace and security in a country where he can grow and fulfil his dreams... Okay, now let's go discuss the matter with Octavio and some others," José added, as he stood up.

Hideout in Guatemala City

After a three-day wait in a small room on the third floor of a rooming house on the corner of two streets in a quiet, relatively uncrowded neighborhood near downtown Guatemala City, Paul was lying fully clothed in a small single bed, staring up at a light bulb on the ceiling, with his right arm resting on his forehead and a book left open, face down, on the bed at his side. All around, deep brown walls seemed to have swallowed the dim light emanating from this single light source, since the curtains of the only window remained close, even in daylight. An old chest of drawers and an upholstered chair, badly worn and torn at the seat and arms, completed the furnishing.

It took him a few seconds to realize that someone might have just knocked on his door. He turned towards it, leaning on one elbow, and waited, listening, wondering if his senses were beginning to play tricks on him. Then, again, a sequence of three discrete knocks, repeated after a short while, and a muffled voice calling, "Miguel, Miguel?"

Recognizing his code name, he leapt to his feet and hurried to open the door to a well-dressed Ladino man in his forties carrying a locked briefcase.

"Miguel?" the man asked again.

"Yes, that's me."

"*Buenos días*, I'm Emiliano," said the man.

"Please, come in."

"May I sit there?" Emiliano asked as he walked towards the old armchair.

"Yes, yes, go ahead."

Having no other seat, Paul sat on the bed.

"Of course, Emiliano is not my real name... just as Miguel isn't yours," the man began, placing the briefcase on his thighs. Then he opened it and took out some documents he handed to Paul, identifying them one after the other: "A fake US passport, an international driver's license and official papers stating the purpose of your trip to Guatemala, including a long-stay visa and a letter from a film production company."

As Paul was looking through the documents, Emiliano went on with his explanation.

"From now on, you are Michael Smith, and you come to do location scouting for the shooting of a feature film. Here's the synopsis," he added, presenting him with a 12-page document.

"You'll be able to give a copy of it if you are asked for details about the project... Basically it's the story of a couple of explorers who discover a Mayan archaeological site. The story also features a volcanic eruption, tomb robbers, and treasure hunters... This will be your justification to travel around the country."

Then Emiliano waited for Paul to look at him before continuing.

"You'll also need to dress accordingly and rent an all-terrain vehicle."

"Okay, but where am I going to get the money for all this?" Paul asked.

"We have opened a bank account in your new name at the

Banco Internacional de Quetzaltenango," answered the man while pulling a thick brown envelope from his inside jacket pocket. "In this envelope you'll find 1,000 U.S. dollars and 5,000 quetzals, as well as your bankbook showing that 140,000 quetzals have been deposited into your account... So, you already have money to spend, and you can start looking for a secluded place to discreetly entertain people from the film community, including perhaps a few celebrities, if you're asked."

After these last explanations, the man stood up, gave Paul the envelope, and handed him a business card.

"Here's the business card of a real estate agent. He will show you a secluded house that we have spotted near Quetzaltenango. He awaits your call."

Overwhelmed by all this information to assimilate at once, Paul stared at the wad of bills he had in one hand.

"But how—"

"Don't ask," the man said, cutting him off.

"When do I start?"

"As soon as you feel ready. The house you're about to visit would be a perfect fit for our needs; it belongs to a Guatemalan diplomat currently posted in Spain. He should feel flattered to rent his main residence to someone working in the film business."

Joy of Reunion

Two weeks later, when Paul came out of the *Banco International* in downtown Quetzaltenango, he was hardly recognizable. He was dressed to match the look of his fake occupation, wearing a cream jacket over a metallic bronze colored shirt with a long-spiked collar sticking out and matching pants whose bottoms rested nonchalantly on shoes of the same color as the shirt. He had shaved, but still hid his face, this time under an ultra-chic urban cap and new Vuarnet sunglasses.

He walked down leisurely to a big caramel Land Rover with slightly tinted windows parked a little further down an adjacent street. As he approached his vehicle, he pulled out his car keys, and started to make them jump in his right hand when another hand sprang up from behind and caught them before they fell back.

Turning around, he found himself facing Mireya. For a split second, he stood there, open-mouthed, and before he could say anything, she kissed him on the cheek and told him to get in the vehicle. She handed him back the keys, got into the passenger seat, and they set off.

Mireya initiated the conversation almost immediately. Staring at Paul's contented grin, she said mockingly, "You seem to have adapted well to your new life."

"It's good to see you again, Mireya. I was told I would be working with you. But it's been over a week since I moved into the residence I was asked to rent and no one has contacted me until today. I was beginning to worry that something might have gone wrong."

"In fact, we've been watching you since your meeting with the realtor. We wanted to make sure that you weren't being followed and that the place was safe. In short, we're ready to move on to the next stage. From now on, I'm officially your new girlfriend, and I'm moving in with you."

Intrigued, Paul casted a questioning glance at her, to which she playfully replied, "You better keep your eyes on the road!"

Suspecting that it was not just mockery, and not wanting to reveal feelings that he had previously thought were forbidden, Paul did not react immediately.

"Of course, it's only a façade," Mireya then added mischievously.

Before the silence grew tense, Paul ended up saying in a jolly tone, "Oh, I have no problem with that. It's just that I was beginning to feel that time was stretching unduly."

"But don't forget that in our relationship, I'm the one who wears the pants. From now on, you are under my command," she said, teasing him again.

"*A sus órdenes, jefe!*" Paul replied, making the military salute.

Shortly after driving up a mountainside, they arrived in front of a massive wooden gate embedded into a concrete wall of more than seven feet high surrounding a large, isolated property overlooking the town of Quetzaltenango. Paul stopped the Land Rover and went to unlock and open the double-leaf door, allowing Mireya to get her first glimpse of the very large single-story house, which awaited them about 50 feet inside the compound. She was especially pleased to see that a wide screened-in veranda ran along the front and sides of the residence.

Massacre

Early in the morning, during a patrol carried out at the beginning of May 1981, some 50 miles from their base camp, a group of twelve rebels, rifles slung over their shoulders, commanded by José, were moving silently on a trail through a small, wooded area on a hilltop, when Octavio, who was leading the way, stopped abruptly at the tree line, dropped to one knee and raised his right hand, ordering the group to stop. José, who was closing the march, hurried to join him, taking care to keep his body bent forward. Without even looking at him, Octavio simply pointed to a village nestled in a small valley at the foot of the hill. Suspicious smoke was rising from the center of the village. José took his binoculars and tried to see if he could detect any activity.

"The place looks deserted. The village has probably been raided."

He scanned the village again, then the surrounding area, making a slow panoramic movement to the left and to the right on the hills that flanked it. The environment resembled that of Concepción, with several small plots of cultivated land on the slopes, crisscrossed by numerous paths and dotted with groves of trees.

After a while, he lowered his binoculars, and said, "Nothing, not a single person in sight. (Then turning to

Octavio) Okay, I'll go down to the village with three men. We'll try to find out what happened there. But first, you and the others will move discreetly on both sides of the village, staying under the cover of the trees. On the way, try to spot the route that any enemies would have taken. on the other side of the village, you will send light signals with a mirror to let us know if the way is clear. My group and I will then start to descend towards the village. You'll do the same when you see us reaching the first houses."

José and his group reached the cemetery at the edge of the village without incident. There they waited for a while, crouching behind tombstones, listening for the slightest noise. Apart from the steady cawing of crows, nothing unusual. After a few minutes, José asked two of his men to weave in and out of the houses along the outer ring road before entering the village at a right angle to the church and heading there. As for them, he and the other member of the group would do the same, going up the street leading from the cemetery to the town square. Then, weapons in hand, they set off, running from house to house, the cawing getting louder as they got closer to the center of the village.

Having reached the back of the last building overlooking the square, José poked his head out to see if they could continue in the open. When he saw the macabre scene that those who had attacked the village had set up in the center of the square, his heart stopped for a second. The bodies of six naked men were hanging there from a makeshift frame, head down, hands and feet bound together. They had been severely beaten and emasculated. Numerous crows were feasting on pieces of flesh while several others swirled around the bodies. The advanced state of decomposition convinced José that the perpetrators of these atrocities had left the area some time ago.

They were finishing untying the bodies when one of the men sent to the church came running. Staring at the bodies lying on the ground with an expression of insanity in his eyes, he ended up saying in a breath, "What a bunch of barbarians! (Then looking up at José) There are more... in the church."

They rushed to the church where they found the other member of the group sitting on the porch steps. The scene the latter had seen inside had left him in a state of deep despondency. There were traces of vomit on the steps in front of him. He had no reaction when José passed by to enter the church. Although the smoke they had seen outside had cleared, a thick veil of ash dust still hung in the nave, and José had to wait a few seconds before he could make out anything in the dim light. As soon as he stepped inside, the smell of dead bodies became so unbearable that he had to cover his nose and mouth with a handkerchief. José then realized the full extent of the drama that had taken place in the village.

Most of the victims were women, children, and elderly people who, thinking they were taking refuge in the church, had instead found themselves trapped inside. Traces of explosives and burning odors indicated that incendiary hand grenades had been used. Those who were still alive had probably been killed with machetes. Wherever he looked in the nave, José could see dismembered bodies and suspicious splashes. It was indeed an act of genocide, the widespread massacre of a group of innocent Mayan Natives.

Infuriated, José stormed out, walked resolutely towards the petrified man still seated, grabbed him by the shoulders and ordered him to get up. Then he turned to the others, who looked overwhelmed and even discouraged. They needed to be shaken up.

"Okay, listen up!" he said. "This is no time to be downhearted. With Octavio and the others, we will track down those bastards to their lair and eliminate them before they strike again elsewhere. Then we'll come back here to properly bury the bodies of our brothers and sisters."

Picking up the Wounded

The Land Rover stopped in front of the same isolated shack in the mountains that had served as a refuge for the members of the CUC during the military raid in Chimaltenango. The landscape beyond the rocky escarpment bathed in the bluish-gray light of dawn. A guerrilla came out of the cabin, rifle slung over his shoulder, and joined Paul who was about to get out of the vehicle.

"We have three injured people inside; one of them is in serious condition."

"Okay, bring them in!"

As the man returned to the cabin, Paul went to open the double door at the back of the SUV. Wearing a Panama hat, a colorful shirt, French pleated jeans, and cowboy boots, he was playing his role of finding locations for a film project perfectly. He had gotten so good at it that soldiers and police officers at roadblocks would salute him as he passed. And Paul made sure to greet them back with the thumbs up. But to get that result, he had previously made several empty passes in the various sectors where most of the safe houses were located and shown his fake ID at checkpoints until he didn't have to. He was now seen as the typical American clumsily trying to fit in with the locals.

Soon, two more guerrillas came out of the refuge carrying a

wounded man on a makeshift stretcher made of branches tied together with ropes. The other two wounded followed, moving on their own: one with his head and left ear bandaged, the other with his right arm in a sling. They sat on the metal benches on both sides of the stretcher that had been slid onto the floor of the vehicle.

Mireya and two orderlies, a man and a woman, were treating some of the wounded lying on cots that had been set up under a marquee made of large canvases tied to tree branches in the courtyard of the clandestine hospital when they heard honking at the gate. They looked at each other, surprised.

"Already?!" wondered Mireya.

"I go see," the man said.

Then they heard honking again.

"That's him! I recognize the sound of the horn."

The man hurried to the gate and opened it. Paul immediately stopped once inside the compound and waited for the man to close and lock the gate.

"We didn't expect you so soon," the man said as he got into the vehicle.

"I have three injured people that I picked up at the first transitional shelter I visited. I decided to bring them back immediately because one of them seems to be in critical condition, Paul explained."

"OK. Let's go straight to the marquee."

Paul turned right to bypass the few trees hiding the place of care. He had not yet finished getting out of the Land Rover that Mireya had already opened the rear door and was greeting the wounded with an encouraging tone.

"*Buenas tardes, compañeros*! Rest assured; you will receive good care here."

She let the men take out the stretcher on which a young boy, who could hardly have been more than fifteen years old, laid unconscious.

"He's my brother," said the man with the bandaged ear who Mireya was helping down.

The new patients were placed side by side on cots. While the orderlies were busy changing the dressings of the less severely injured, Mireya took care of the teenager. She began by cutting off the rudimentary bandage wrapping his torso and then gently lifted it up. She frowned as she discovered a deep wound, probably caused by shrapnel. She gently pressed the edge of the wound, causing a stream of blood to gush out. Then, with a worried look, she began to clean it, before applying an antiseptic cream. Throughout the procedure, her patient moaned weakly while remaining unconscious. She ended her exam by placing a hand on the teenager's forehead, then turned to Paul who was waiting nervously at the foot of the bed.

"He's feverish and I think he's suffering from internal bleeding."

"Too bad Charles Ramsay isn't with us."

"He couldn't come anyway. You told me that he was always accompanied by two secret agents acting as bodyguards. I'll call Dr. Romero; he's a surgeon who supports our cause. We have been instructed to call on him only in extreme emergencies... and I'm sure that's the case here," said Mireya, looking again at her young patient. "I hope he can come immediately."

She asked Paul to apply a damp compress to the boy's forehead and to remain with him while she made the call.

"What if he wakes up?"

"If that happens and he asks for water, you give him some but only small sips. Hold his hand and talk to him. Tell him he will be okay," she added before heading for the house.

Unsure of how to handle such a situation, Paul watched Mireya leave the marquee with some apprehension. He dipped a washcloth in the bucket of water placed near the bed, wrung it, and approached the patient. As soon as he applied the compress to the youngster's forehead, the latter opened his feverish eyes.

"*Padre?*" he ended up mumbling, staring at the face bent over him.

Caught off guard, Paul automatically looked behind him, unrealistically hoping for Mireya's return, then he leaned over a little more and said softly, "I'm not a priest, but a friend."

"*Perdóname padre* for I have sinned... I killed a man," the boy added as if he hadn't heard Paul's voice.

Understanding what was happening, the man lying on the next bed decided to intervene.

"*Oye, compañero!*" he called out in a hoarse voice. Paul turned to him.

"He's my younger brother Pablito. I think he's going to die. I beg you. Please, pretend you're a priest. Give him your blessing."

This call and the importance of the moment prompted Paul to take charge. He knelt to get close to the boy's head. Then, placing a hand on his forehead, he took a moment to reflect, and began to say a prayer for the dying.

"O merciful Jesus, You who burn with an ardent love for souls, I implore You in the name of the agony of Your Holy Heart and the pains of Your Immaculate Mother, to purify by

Your Most Precious Blood, Pablito who is in agony. Amen!"

The prayer seemed to have soothed the young Pablito, who finally closed his eyes. His brother, with tears in the eyes, nodded approvingly. Mireya, who had returned during the prayer, watched Paul getting up and making the sign of the cross. Then turning around, he saw in Mireya's sad look that she had probably witnessed a good part of the scene. She was now looking at him with tenderness. A little embarrassed, he went to join her while keeping his eyes fixed on the ground.

"Is the doctor coming?"

"I haven't been able to reach him. He's in surgery. I'll try again a little later."

"Is there anyone else?"

"Unfortunately not. He's the only surgeon in the area we can rely on."

They both looked again at the injured boy, knowing that he probably didn't have long to live.

That night, Paul could not fall asleep. Lying on his back with his eyes wide open, he was unable to stop the continuous stream of images and thoughts spinning in his head. The haggard face and feverish eyes of the young Pablito imploring him to absolve him of his sins before he died, mingled with those of Jorge and the other youngsters from Concepción, alive and dead. After a while, it was Mireya's face, caressing his cheek on the boat in the shadow of the volcano, that popped up. The tenderness of her gaze was indelibly etched in his mind. He had felt the same when he had caught her watching him with the young Pablito. For the first time, he thought that there was perhaps more there than tenderness and compassion. Was it love? The more he thought about it, the more he understood that he had unconsciously rejected that possibility. Captivated by those big velvety coffee-colored eyes, his mind calmed down and he quickly fell asleep.

Attack on the Rebel Camp

A few days after the collection and evacuation of the victims, as the ruins of the ancient Mayan city of Utatlan were taking on a golden-brown hue under the rising sun, the aura of peaceful and timeless beauty radiating from the surrounding landscape was suddenly corrupted by the sound of running footsteps accompanied by loud breathing and whipping branches. Blowing like a locomotive, Octavio soon appeared at the end of the trail he and Paul had taken to get to the rebel camp. He stopped at the edge of the ravine, looked back, and held his breath, listening for unusual sounds. People were coming fast. He skidded down the steep slope to the bottom of the ravine, which was just beginning to emerge from the gloom. Without stopping, he was back speeding up.

Halfway to the Utatlan side, he stopped abruptly when hearing helicopter rotors arriving at high speed. He looked up just in time to see three military choppers hurtling toward the rebel camp. Immediately afterwards, indistinct shouts rang out behind him. Looking over his shoulder, he saw that his pursuers had reached the end of the path to the ravine and were pointing their guns at him. Realizing that he could not escape them, he decided to surrender. But they shot him before he could raise his hands above his head.

By the time the lookouts perched in the trees at the edge of the forest saw the low-flying helicopters coming rapidly toward them, it was already too late to raise the alarm. The whirlybirds began firing rockets immediately after passing over them, as if they did not know exactly where the camp was located but knew they were heading in the right direction. In fact, it was the sound of explosions, rapidly closing on the camp that alerted those who were there at the time, spreading fear and panic among them. While most ran around trying to save as much as they could before fleeing again, some took their rifles and pointed them skyward. Soon the rockets reached the surrounding woods, then the camp, and the whole place went up in flames.

Bad News

The patients had just finished eating, and Paul, with two orderlies, had started to collect the meal trays. As he approached young Pablito's now unoccupied bed, Paul felt his heart clench as he thought back to the previous day's scene. But the little nod that his brother gave him from the next bed acted like a balm, comforting him in his impression of doing useful work. And it is with a lighter heart that Paul entered the kitchen with trays and dishes to wash.

He was about to go back for more trays when Mireya, who was working at keeping the books in a nearby room, called him in. Seeing that he remained standing at her door, she beckoned him in and pointed to the transistor radio placed at one end of her desk.

"They just announced there will be breaking news coverage about a military offensive against insurgents in the El Quiché District near Santa Cruz del Quiché," she explained before increasing the volume of the radio.

The newscaster returned on air, only to give way almost immediately to a government spokesman, who began his speech by declaring in a professional and enthusiastic tone that the Guatemalan army was engaged in a heroic battle to safeguard the freedom of the country's inhabitants against communist terrorists. He then mentioned that it was a major operation requiring the use of armored vehicles with the deployment of ground and air troops and that intense fighting had already taken place in the city of Santa Cruz and around the ancient Mayan site of Utatlan.

Paul and Mireya looked at each other, alarmed by the threat that it posed to their friends. As they continued to listen in horror to the rest of the story, they were outraged when hearing the spokesman accuse Cuban nationals of having exploited the naivety of the native people to prompt them to take up arms against the state by spreading falsehoods.

At that moment, the phone rang three times and stopped. They both stared at the device until it rang two more times and then stopped again.

"It's for me," Paul said. "I've got to go."

"Wait!" insisted Mireya. She came over to him, kissed him on the cheek, and urged him to be careful and keep a cool head.

"Don't worry, they know me around there."

When Paul arrived at the location of a new transitional shelter, this time in a wooded hilly area, there was another vehicle of the same type as his parked alongside the cabin. As he passed behind the other vehicle, Paul noticed that six injured were already inside, packed like sardines. He nodded to the driver, who was about to close the rear doors and looking at him despondently. The latter pointed with his head to the shelter where many other wounded, leaning against a wall, waited to be evacuated, and said that there were more inside.

Among those outside, Paul immediately spotted José, sitting against the wall near the front door. His friend was staring blankly while holding his son Arturo in his arms. The latter had his head and arms bandaged and seemed to be unconscious. As helpers were beginning to carry the injured to the Land Rover, Paul quickly went to José. Although the latter did not react to his presence, Paul was relieved to see that Arturo was breathing well. He put a hand on José's right shoulder and pressed it slightly. José looked up, and his eyes became clouded with tears as he recognized his friend. When asked if he was hurt, José nodded no, then, unable to speak, he looked down at his son.

Paul thought about asking what had happened to the other members of his family, but it was not the right time. Instead, he held out a hand to help him up.

"Come on, José. We'll take good care of Arturo."

Maya Sacred Calendar

By late afternoon, the clandestine hospital was already filled with new patients and half a dozen orderlies were moving back and forth between the house and the marquee. Sitting at the bedside of his son Arturo, resting in a cot a little apart from the others at one end of the veranda, José seemed to have regained his senses after having been reassured about his child's state of health. The latter was sleeping soundly while his father kept his attention focused on drawing something in a small notebook with colored pencils.

Paul had just completed his third and final casualty transport. Mireya managed to intercept him as he was hurrying to his friend. She told him that José's wife and mother had died during the attack on the rebel camp. Paul took a moment to digest the terrible news. He did not want to get too emotional when approaching his friend. Still bending over his paper pad, José looked up when he heard footsteps getting closer. He greeted Paul with a sad smile, then pointing to his son, he said, "Mireya promised me a quick recovery with no after-effects."

"It broke my heart when I heard about Anna and your mother," Paul said, putting a friendly hand on José's shoulder.

"They attacked while most of the men had left the camp to go on patrol. When I returned with my group just before sunset, we found a scene of total devastation. Arturo was incredibly lucky. I found him under Anna..." Suddenly assailed by the memory, José stopped talking. His eyes misted up and he bit his lower lip to hold back his tears. Then, looking up at Paul, he cleared his throat to add with a tremulous voice, "At first I thought that he too was dead."

She did everything she could to save him, and she succeeded," Paul said, emphasizing Anna's courage. Then he asked, "What about Luis?"

"He probably managed to escape, or we would have found him," José said with a glint of hope in his eyes.

"That sounds very encouraging. But you haven't mentioned Manuel yet. Do you know what happened of him?"

José remained silent for a moment, his gaze lost in the distance, and then spoke with a firmer, deeper voice.

"Two weeks ago, while on patrol in the Totonicapán area, we came across a small, isolated village. The place seemed to have been deserted, but a plume of black smoke rising from the center of the village intrigued us. So, we decided to go and have a closer look at what it meant. When we arrived at the public square, we found six men hanged by their feet and emasculated. Most of the inhabitants had taken refuge in the church, probably believing that they were safe from violence because of its sacredness. (Then glancing at Paul with a look haunted by memory) The attackers barricaded them in and threw incendiary grenades through the windows. Those who survived the explosions were finished off with machetes...

... While those who left their villages to fight, the death squads are using scorched earth tactics. They raid villages to destroy crops and slaughter those who remained there, mostly women, children, and the elderly ... When I told Manuel about what happened in Totonicapán, he decided to go back to

Concepción, saying his place was there, among the elders. Before leaving, he also told me that he had taught me everything he knew and that it was now my duty to do the same with Arturo, so that he could become a leader and a shaman."

"What will you do?"

"When Arturo gets better, I will take him to the Cuchumatanes mountains and try to cross into Mexico. I have to do everything I can to save my son, so that he can grow up in a safer environment." I don't want to stay here any longer. I think the military knew where to find us when they attacked our camp. The noose is tightening around us. You too should leave while you still can."

"I can't just walk away and leave the injured. But if you think you've been betrayed or that someone has spoken under torture, you should raise those thoughts with Mireya," Paul replied.

"I did. She said she would contact David to discuss it with him."

Still uncomfortable with the idea of abandoning the injured, Paul wanted to lighten the mood.

"When I came to see you, I saw you doodling something."

"I was drawing a calendar," José said, showing it to Paul.

"Is this the one you call the Sacred Calendar?"

"Yes. We called it *Tzolk'in*, which can be translated as the distribution of the days. That's the one we use to determine the time of religious and ceremonial events. It is composed of two cycles, one of 20 named days associated with a picture or glyph with a distinct meaning, and one of 13 numbered days, each of which continuously repeats just like two-gear wheels with 20 and 13 teeth. It takes 260 days for the two cycles to realign on the beginning day of each cycle (260 = 20 x 13), so the Sacred

Round has 260 days."

Paul pointed to one of the symbols in the drawing.

"It looks like a frog."

"Good point," José said. "The frog is used to indicate when the waters are going to recede or when they have receded depending on the other symbols with which it is associated. There are different ways of interpreting this statement. For example, according to Manuel, we are coming to the end of a long cycle of about 400 years, which would mark the transition from a period of great darkness to a new age of enlightenment and progress for the Mayas."

José took out the page on which he had drawn the calendar.

"This one is for you, so you can practice deciphering it."

"Wow, thanks José. I'll treasure it."

"It always feels good to draw the calendars. It allows me to situate what is happening in a wider context and reconsider our decisions accordingly."

Later that evening, when most of the wounded were already asleep, Paul was sitting at the kitchen table, trying to match the calendar symbols and glyphs José had drawn with their meanings written on another sheet. At times, he would glance at Mireya, who was talking to someone on the phone in a nearby room. He could not hear what she was saying, but her face showed that it was serious business. When she hung up, he put the drawing down and watched her come to him with a grim look on her face.

"Is there a problem?" Paul asked.

"In the afternoon, I called David to discuss the situation. He just called back. He said that people previously associated with the CUC have been arrested. These people are not directly linked to us, but if they talk, they can compromise others closer to us."

"My goodness. Then we'd have to find a new location and evacuate everyone, Paul worried, seriously alarmed by the prospect."

"That's why all the regional leaders are called to an emergency meeting tomorrow at dawn in the capital. I want you to come with me. We will probably discuss the situation regarding the transition houses, and you're best positioned to comment on this... Plus I don't like the idea of driving alone at night."

"Don't worry. I want to go. Besides, you seem to forget that the Land Rover was rented under my fake name, so I have to go."

"Right," Mireya said. Then, glancing at the calendar drawing, she added mockingly, "Do you intend to become a shaman and follow in José's footsteps?"

Caught off guard, Paul folded the sheet of paper and slipped it into his shirt pocket. "I just want to understand the people better, how they see things."

"I'm teasing you... We should go to bed now. We'll have to get up early."

"Ok! But before, I want to tell José about the meeting, even if I have to wake him up."

Surrender!

The Land Rover's headlights pierced the thick, dark veil of a starless night. Since their departure from Quetzaltenango, Paul and Mireya had remained silent, lost in their thoughts. With their eyes wide open, they looked like two owls, their gaze fixed on the little they could see of the Pan-American Highway. They emerged from their torpor only when the glow of the capital city lights appeared in the distance.

Paul looked at Mireya and said, "You know, when I talked to José last night, he didn't say much, but I saw a real sense of urgency in his eyes."

Mireya kept her eyes on the road without commenting.

"By the way, I didn't ask you what you think of José's intention to go to Mexico," Paul added, intrigued by Mireya's silence.

"Look, he almost lost his whole family. I understand that he must make sure that Arturo lives in a safe environment while the country is in turmoil. And he's not the only one who has considered crossing the border. Many, perhaps thousands, have already done so," Mireya finally said. Then, glancing quickly at Paul, she challenged him by asking, "And you, are you thinking of leaving too?"

Paul took some time to think, and then, "Maybe. I'll see after the meeting. If, we can't save the hospital or establish another one, I think I might go with José, if he agrees. And I think you should come too. I would love it if you would."

"I don't want to disappoint you, but I wouldn't be surprised if José was already gone when we get back from Guatemala City."

Paul gave her a puzzled look, then stared back at the road ahead.

"All is not lost yet, you know. There are still hundreds of combatants in the hills, not counting those in the Peten jungle," Mireya added, analyzing the situation from a different perspective.

Primarily concerned with the fate of their wounded, Paul went on, "I think you should rather try to negotiate a truce with the government. When I met Charles Ramsay on my return to Guatemala, he told me that some members of the government did not agree with the actions of the army and especially not with the crimes committed by the death squads, who can act with impunity. I could contact him, he knows people."

"Good idea. I'll suggest to David that we bring this up at the meeting. He told me that some of ORPA's leaders will be there... We'll know better after the meeting."

The meeting took place in a two-story house in a quiet residential area not far from the downtown core of the capital. To avoid drawing attention, the participants had parked their vehicles along the neighboring streets. Inside the house, the discussion had already begun. Paul, Mireya, David, a Spanish priest, two guerrilla leaders (a man and a woman) and a Cuban observer were sitting around a table. During the discussion, Paul could not help but cast worried glances at the adjoining living room where two guerrillas armed with AK-47 assault rifles were keeping watch behind a large window. He refocused his attention on the debate when the issue of the injured was raised. David came forward with a solution.

"We could set up makeshift hospitals in the Peten jungle, and in the meantime, the injured could be sent to our shelters in the nearby mountains."

"Yes, but if our facilities are compromised, as you fear, the shelters may well be too. Besides, if we decide to move the injured to the jungle, it means that we will have to abandon the most serious cases... My surgeon friend who is helping us in Quetzaltenango won't want to follow us into the jungle, even in the hills," Mireya countered.

"We can't leave anyone behind, and we can't send them to a regular hospital. If the police get their hands on them, they will not hesitate to use torture to make them talk. It's just way too risky," the Cuban observer added.

They were suddenly interrupted by one of the guerrillas, who shouted "*Soldados!*"

Paul and the Spanish priest looked at each other, stunned, while everyone else rushed into the living room to peek through the window.

Outside, soldiers were taking up positions in the street, while police officers began knocking on nearby doors to ask people to evacuate. Police-guarded security cordons had been set up a few hundred feet on either side of the street and on both sides of the nearest intersection to hold back passersby and neighbors who had been asked to leave their homes.

The Cuban observer put a hand on the shoulder of one of the armed guerrillas.

"Don't shoot. Let them think that we don't know they are there. Wait and see where they take up position."

Hidden behind the wall of a house at the corner of the intersection to the left of the rebel house, a military officer was listening to a foreign civilian, who was hiding his face under a hat pulled down over his forehead and sunglasses.

"Don't forget! We want you to take them alive, at least some of them."

"I'll give them the opportunity to surrender first. But I can't guarantee the outcome if they start shooting at my men," the officer replied.

Then the latter came forward in the open, exposing only his face, to check the readiness of his men. Soldiers equipped with M16 assault rifles and rocket launchers were positioned along the walls and on the roofs of the houses next to the insurgents'. He looked behind him to see an armored vehicle with a 105mm mobile gun approaching. He signaled the vehicle to stop and wait. Satisfied, the officer raised the megaphone he carried in his right hand to his mouth.

"This is Captain Fernandez of the Guatemalan army. I am addressing the occupants of the house located at *35 Calle 10-14*. We know you are there and who you are. You have fifteen minutes to surrender. If you have not surrendered to us within the time allowed, we will attack. There will be no other warning. You have no chance to escape. You are surrounded... Surrender!"

Inside the rebels' house, the Cuban observer took things in hand. He went to open a hidden door in the kitchen and came back in the living room, carrying five more AK-47 assault rifles. He gave one to each group leader, as well as to David and Mireya. He ordered the two guerrillas in the living room to stay there, and then asked Mireya and the other two leaders to go upstairs and take up positions at the front windows, while he and David would go to the back of the house to avoid being attacked from behind. But before they could take up their defensive positions, David demanded that everyone hand over their identification papers.

As she was about to go upstairs, Mireya turned to Paul, who was watching her. Their eyes merged for a moment. They nodded in unison, and she went up. Then David approached Paul and the Spanish priest who, not knowing what to do, had remained at the table. He placed all the identification papers and two pistols in front of them. Both looked at the weapons in horror, suspecting full well what they implied.

"I know that you will not want to shoot at the enemy. I'm giving you these handguns because we can't let them take us alive... for the sake of our brothers and sisters," David told them. Then pointing to the documents, "As for the papers, burn them."

Before rushing to join the Cuban observer at the back of the house, David turned to the guerrillas in the living room and shouted, "*Viva la revolución Guatemalteca!*"

The two guerrillas reacted by repeating the war cry, then broke the windows and started shooting. They were immediately followed by those upstairs targeting the soldiers on the roofs. The enemy returned fire, and bullets began to fly and whistle all around. Taking the pistols and identity papers with them, Paul and the priest went to sit on the floor in a corner of the kitchen. They put the papers in a large pot and burned them.

After about fifteen minutes of intense fire from both sides

and seeing some of his men hit, Captain Fernandez lost patience.

"They won't surrender, and I don't want to have more casualties," he said to the foreign civilian.

He came out of the corner of the house from where he was monitoring the scene and sounded two long whistle blasts, signaling his men to stop shooting and take cover. The firing on the army side ceased and the soldiers with rocket launchers stepped forward to take up firing positions. The captain then motioned to the driver of the armored vehicle to enter the battle. The vehicle started moving heavily, turned left onto *Calle 10-14* and slowly made its way toward the insurgents' house.

When the guerrillas in the living room realized that the enemy had stopped firing and was now out of sight, they stopped shooting and looked at each other, puzzled. Then they heard the engine of a heavy vehicle.

Seeing it coming toward them, they shouted, "*Ataque de tanque!*" and started shooting at it.

Paul and the priest looked at each other, understanding that this could be the end. The priest made the Sign of the Cross, then blessed Paul and began a prayer. Paul took the calendar José had given him from his shirt pocket and unfolded it to take a last look at it. As he reflected on the path he had taken, he felt at peace with himself, ready to face his fate. He was about to burn the calendar when there was a huge blast, and everything vanished in a big white flash.

Epilogue

Comfortably ensconced in a sun lounger, legs under a blanket, on the rear balcony of his congregation's retirement home, Father Callaghan was enjoying basking under a lovely blue sky and a hot, mid-September sun. From there, he had an enviable view on an old forest of giant pines stretching out to his left and facing him, a beautiful cemetery, very well maintained, where members of his congregation had been laid to rest since the nineteenth century, including some very young novices who died from being sick in the early years. Father Callaghan thought it was an ideal setting to feel humble before the All, the Great spiritual Reality.

He was about to doze off when a novice arrived with an envelope from the Foreign Mission Society. He thanked the young man and, intrigued by the unusual nature of the letter, opened it with some trepidation. He unfolded the one-page letter bearing the signature of the Brother Superior General of the Foreign Missions Society. A quick first reading left him shocked and dismayed. He began to read it again, this time more slowly.

"I am sorry I have to inform you of the death of our volunteer and humanitarian coworker Paul Desilets. His death occurred in obscure circumstances on *Calle 10–14* in Guatemala City on August 29th of current year.

According to a spokesman for the presidential palace in Guatemala City, Paul Desilets, designated as an American missionary, was killed in a clash between military forces and a group of leftist guerrillas. According to the official, our young compatriot was not just an innocent bystander caught in the crossfire, but a guerrilla commander operating under the nom de guerre of *Comandante* Miguel.

The Chargé d'Affaires at the American Embassy in Guatemala echoed the government's claim by suggesting that Desilets had been caught flagrante delicto."

The letter also said that Paul Desilets would have been identified by another person who knew him and worked in Guatemala.

Still holding the letter in his hand, Father Callaghan let his arm fall back on his thigh. His gaze wandered for a moment, then his eyes moistened as he thought back to the last two years and saw the innocent enthusiasm on Paul's face again. Curiously, the same quote from the Gospel of John that had come to Paul's mind on Christmas Eve came to him: "There is no greater love than to lay down one's life for one's friends."

A few weeks later, in Guatemala, while the day had dawned a few hours earlier over the Peten jungle, the highest pyramid of the Tikal complex, still in semi-darkness, was beginning to emerge in the light as the sun continued to rise above the canopy and the haunting cries of the howler monkeys echoed from everywhere.

Calmly settled inside their nesting hole dug high up in a tall avocado tree on the edge of the rainforest, a pair of Quetzal birds became concerned when the screeching suddenly stopped. For a moment, the silence seemed deafening, then the echo of machete blows cutting through vines began to be heard. Puzzled by this unusual noise, the male Quetzal left his tree and flew toward the pyramid. He landed on the roof comb of the huge structure from where he waited to see if what was about to come out of the forest could pose a threat.

The sun's rays had just reached the bottom of the pyramid when a group of eight guerrillas emerged from the forest and began to file across the plaza. They were dressed simply, with nonmatching worn clothing—jeans, colorful long-sleeved shirts, bandanas around the neck, and caps on their head—and running shoes or work boots. They were all armed with AK-47 assault rifles and wore no distinctive signs indicating that they belonged to the guerrilla.

As they walked past the pyramid, the male Quetzal gave his warning cry: 'koy-koy-koy-koy' followed by rapid 'kwah-kwah-kwah.' Then he left his perch and swooped over the guerrillas. Upon hearing the Quetzal's cry, all the guerrillas looked up to see the long, iridescent blue-green tail of Guatemala's national bird glistening in the sun. When the third man in line took off his cap to get a better see the bird, it revealed the face of José's brother, Luis.

The Quetzal continued to bugle until the group had disappeared into the forest on the other side of the plaza.

Acknowledgments

The preparation and research for *Blood for Freedom* would not have been possible without the help and guidance of many friends and relatives.

First, of course, my thanks go to Peter McFarlane, author of *Northern Shadows*, for his participation in the field research in Guatemala and Mexico and his collaboration in the development of the script.

Marc G. LeVasseur MAT, PhD in Humanities, who served as my consultant editor.

Thanks to my primary supporters and first readers: Gabriel Thibault, Réjean Désilets, Guy Piché and Raymond Piché, and Catherine Proulx.

Finally, and most important, my thanks to my wife Céline for her support, understanding, and patience in the long months I labored on this book.